OH JOE

OH JOE

MICHAEL Z. LEWIN

FIVE STAR

A part of Gale, Cengage Learning

GALE
CENGAGE Learning

Detroit • New York • San Francisco • New Haven, Conn • Waterville, Maine • London

Set in 11 pt. Plantin.
Printed on permanent paper.

LIBRARY OF CONGRESS CATALOGING-IN-PUBLICATION DATA

Lewin, Michael Z.
  Oh Joe / Michael Z. Lewin. — 1st ed.
     p. cm.
  ISBN-13: 978-1-59414-667-1 (alk. paper)
  ISBN-10: 1-59414-667-5 (alk. paper)
  1. Murder—Fiction. 2. Indianapolis (Ind.)—Fiction. I. Title.
PS3562.E929036 2008
813'.54—dc22   2008016795

First Edition. First Printing: July 2008.

Published in 2008 in conjunction with Tekno Books and Ed Gorman.

Printed in the United States of America
1 2 3 4 5 6 7 12 11 10 09 08

This book is for Aimee, Simon and Roger.

1

I bet some people would say it was all Kelly's fault for leaving me alone in the first place. For sure, it wouldn't of happened if she'd stood up to her witch of a mom to say if I didn't go to the funeral then none of us would. Kelly's mom could perfectly well of taken me along. Or just loaned me the money. If not for me then because of Little Joe and how a boy needs his father, especially if he is young. Even a witch of a mom ought to know about that and make allowance.

But Kelly didn't stand up, probably because her mom hates me so bad, and it was her mom's own dad that was getting buried, even if they weren't close.

I'm not perfect—fair enough, I put my hand up. But who is? Truth is, there are guys out there a whole lot worse than me. A whole lot. George for one.

So the way it all happened was Kelly and Little Joe went to the funeral, and I didn't, which was scheduled for four days. And when Kelly came home the day earlier what she found sure wasn't the way it ought to of been. I shouldn't of been doing what I was doing, but it all came from me not going to the funeral. If I'd gone to the funeral then we'd of been together and Kelly wouldn't of screamed the place down and left with Little Joe for her mom's apartment. And if Kelly didn't leave, then I wouldn't of been in Berringers when George came in.

And so many things would have been different if that didn't happen. Way different. Way better.

So I was sitting in Berringers, talking to a girl named Melody. Which I would never of been doing if Kelly'd been at home instead of walking out the door cursing blue murder.

Truth is, Berringers is where I met Kelly in the first place, even if she and her friend were only fifteen at the time. Berringers is where I go when I don't have someplace else I ought to be. It's almost a family thing, because my pa used to come to Berringers until he died. He came there from so far back they had a turtle pond then to raise turtles for soup, that's how long ago, though the pond's a flower garden now.

And Melody seemed to understand all I was going through, with Kelly walking out and a boy needing his father, no matter how young. Yes, she did. Not the prettiest face in the world, Melody, but the rest of her would go a long way. And she was being real understanding, which I appreciated, because I wasn't about to get any from Kelly anytime soon.

What happened was that Melody went to take a few minutes in the ladies' room. I sipped from my beer and dipped a wing, and looked up at the TV where they had the local news. I remember they were talking about how Indianapolis was having a wave of murders. Six in the last week alone. Course the weather was hot—the time was late July and hot's about all you can expect in Indy then, apart from humidity.

On the TV they said people were doing crazy things. Well, they didn't need to tell me that, because I had the example of Kelly. Not that what I did was right. But running away to her witch of a mom's place wasn't going to solve it, was it?

Maybe, I remember thinking, maybe when it cools down she'll come back. And it was at that very minute that I felt this hand on my shoulder. I turned around and George Wayne was standing there with this big, dumb grin on his face, bold as brass. "Joseph," he said, "as I live and breathe. I swear I was hoping I'd run into you here tonight. I swear it."

"You were, huh?" He had a funny red mark on the side of his face, like somebody hit him, but I didn't ask about it at the time because I thought it could of been a disease he had nowadays and it wouldn't be polite.

"It's been a long time," George said. "A long time. Man!" He smiled like we were still uninterrupted buddies. He patted the bar a couple of times and sat down. "How long's it been? A year?"

"Two years in October."

"That long? Man!" He gave Eileen behind the bar a wave. "Double Jack on the rocks, and another of whatever my man Joe here is having."

"No thanks," I said, but George ignored me and so did Eileen.

Truth is, I didn't know if Melody would want another drink when she came back or whether she was just getting herself ready for us to get out of here. Oh well.

"So, how you doing, man?" George asked. "How's business?"

My business is a truck that I got when I was lucky on the lotto eleven years ago. I use it to do house clearances, furniture moving, that kind of thing. "It's OK," I said, though it has its ups and downs. "You want something moved? Is that what you were looking for me for?"

He laughed and said, "Not exactly," and patted me on the back. "And what about that little girl you used to be with? What was her name? The blonde one with the big tits and the buck teeth. She still in the picture?"

"Kelly," I said.

"Yeah, that's it. Kelly. A real piece of ass, that one."

"Which one?" but this was Melody, suddenly talking over my other shoulder. "Who you talking about? You talking about me?

9

Because I'll tell you what you can do with your 'piece of ass' talk, Mr. Joe Prince. You can stick it up your piece of ass, that's what you can do with it."

"No, Melody," I said. "I didn't say anything about you. It's this jerk here—"

But she was already scooping up her stuff. "Asshole," she said. She let the screen door bang as she went out and everything.

"Thanks a lot, George."

"Hey, sorry, man, sorry. I didn't know."

"Is there one single time that you being around hasn't screwed things up for me? One single time?"

It wasn't a real question, though, because George and I went back a long way. Just about all the way. It was in high school together from the time of being freshmen. There were half a dozen of us back then. And a couple of those—Chuckie and Max—I was even in grade school with first. So somewhere in all those years there must of been something George didn't screw up for me. I just couldn't remember any.

He said, "You do know, don't you, Joe, that I never meant for you to go down the drain last time."

"I was lucky to get off with time served and a fine. Some other judge and I could still be inside."

"I know, I know, man." He shook his head. "At least you're out, though, eh?"

"I still had to find the money for the fine. And I sure don't remember you leaving any help in my mailbox."

"I couldn't stay in town. You knew that."

George had this plan for scamming gas stations that required the help of a shill. The judge accepted that I didn't know what I was doing. Truth is, I didn't know what I was doing, not the whole of it. An old friend—someone you palled around with in high school—he asks you to do him some favors . . . What are you going to do? Well, at least I learned my damn lesson. It didn't matter what George was looking for me to do now, I wasn't going to do him more favors. No sirree. The only favor I'd do for George Wayne was let him pay me back the two thousand bucks for the fine. He could do that for me, if he wanted to. Only, now that I thought about it, truth is, it was Kelly who found most of the money for that fine. I only had about a hundred and seventy at the time. Maybe if I got it back from George and took it to her at her mother's . . .

George was saying, "I see you still got your way with the ladies, Joseph."

But what were the chances of getting money back from George?

"It's always like a damn revolving door at your place."

"What?" I said.

"I was saying how you were always the one with the ladies."

"I just don't like to sleep alone." And it's true, I don't. After a day or two alone I just feel . . . I don't know. Not whole. "Look, George . . ."

"What?"

"That fine was two thousand dollars. How about you pay me back?"

"Two grand? That much?"

"That much."

"Hey, Joseph, you know I'd give it to you if I had it, don't you?"

"No," I said. "I don't know any such thing. I bet you got that much in each sock, only truth is, you don't ever intend to pay me back." George was always one for carrying cash.

"I don't have it, Joe. Honest. I'm a straight arrow now. I've learned my lesson. I really have."

"That'll be the day."

"It is the day."

11

"Whatever you say."

"You didn't used to be so cynical, Joe. You used to look on the bright side."

"And look where it got me."

"It got you your own business and . . . Hell, I don't know. What else?" He downed most of his bourbon and waved again to Eileen to order us another round of drinks. "Come on, drink up," he said. "There's another one coming."

I was about to say I didn't want one, but then I realized I did. Pity about Melody. Looked like another night alone. I drank up.

"So what did happen to that little Kelly?" George asked. "I thought she'd been around for a long time and you said that she was different. Didn't you get married to her, or something?"

"We had a kid." It hit me then how much I missed Little Joe too.

"That was it," George said. "You knocked her up. I knew there was something." Eileen brought the drinks.

"And now she's left me," I said.

"What?"

"Kelly left me."

"Oh, that's too bad. How long ago was that?"

"Last night."

"Oh, fuck. Sorry, man." Then he grinned. "And now you're back in Berringers, casting your line. Or should I say your rod?" He laughed and shook his head. "You just can't help yourself, can you, Joseph?"

Truth is, I can't. Truth is, if there was a twelve-step program, or something like that, I'd take it.

It's not like Kelly doesn't know it about me. That's one of the different things about her, she understands me, what I need. And as long as she's there, I'm fine, she takes care of it, we're good, even if her understanding does get tired sometimes.

What set Kelly off this time was how she felt she had to go away for the four days to her grandfather's funeral in Vegas. We even talked about how it might be a problem, and how bad I wanted to go with her too, though I didn't know where I was going to get the money for the ticket. But when her witch of a mother put her foot down about me not coming, Kelly told me, she said, "Grow up, Joe. You're twenty-seven years old. You've got to be able to take care of yourself for just four days."

Only it wasn't the days that were the problem. It was the nights.

I got through two of them, but then I said to myself, I'll go down to Berringers, just for a drink, just for the conversation. But it didn't work out that way.

There was this little redhead named . . . Damn, what was her name? And one drink led to another and then Kelly came back a day early because she was wanting to be there for me, and there was the redhead and me, all flagrant.

Damn.

Kelly, she's not wrong. I ought to grow up. I ought to be better. I'm not a kid anymore. I sure do miss her.

"Joe?" George was saying.

I said, "I ought to be stronger. I know I ought to. But I'm not."

"She catch you with some woman? That it?"

"Yeah."

"So, she's not coming back? That what you're saying?"

"That's what she's saying." I sure hoped she was going to change her mind. I hoped maybe a couple days living with her witch of a mom would be about all she could bear.

"Because," George was saying, "if you're free at the moment, then maybe there's a way we can help each other out."

If it hadn't of been for the situation with Kelly, there is no way—no way—I would of agreed to do any damn thing with George Wayne, not even if he was offering to pay me three hundred, in cash up front and completely legal. But . . . Three hundred may not be two grand, but if I had three hundred in my hand, at least then Kelly would see that I was trying my best to work hard for her and Little Joe. And three hundred isn't nothing. Not even the witch could say that three hundred was nothing.

But it wasn't even the money that really tipped it. It was that if I did what George wanted I was guaranteed to be out of harm's temptation from women at the same time.

And what I thought was that if maybe I could go for the three whole days—and nights—then maybe it would be like giving up cigarettes where the first few days are the hardest. And I thought if I did that, it might show Kelly how much I wanted to try to grow up like she wanted and how much I wanted her back.

Because what George wanted me to do was to live by myself for three days out in the middle of Geist Reservoir on a houseboat.

"On a what?"

"Even from way back," he said, "I always wanted to live out at Geist."

I didn't remember anything like that, but I didn't say it. I drank from the beer he bought me instead.

"Well," George said, "now I do live out at Geist, just not on the shore."

Geist Reservoir is a big artificial lake they made back in the forties for the water. Only then they started selling the land around it to rich people and these days it's one of the fanciest areas in town—well on the edge of town. It's way out northeast. I said, "I don't ever remember seeing any houseboats out there."

"Mine's the only one," George said.

"Oh."

"And they don't like it."

"Who doesn't?"

"The fat cats all around who think just because they paid a couple zillion for their damn houses, I shouldn't have the right to sit in the middle of the lake for free. But damn it, Joe, I'm a native Hoosier-American. If I don't have a right to float my boat on good Hoosier water, I don't know who does." He pounded his fist on the bar.

Eileen turned to look. She doesn't like Berringers to be a rough place so she frowned. Maybe it not being rough is why women feel comfortable coming there alone. That and because Eileen makes them welcome and not feel like whores.

George was saying, "They think they own the water, not just the land. But the water's God's and the State of Indiana's."

"I can see that," I said.

"I've been out there nearly four months now." George downed his bourbon. "I've been anchored the same place the whole time, not getting in anybody's way. I don't bother the fishermen. I don't play loud music. The sailboats have plenty of deep water either side to go around me. What's the harm?"

I shrugged.

"But some of them, they can't stand it. They send their kids out to race their speedboats back and forth to make waves and rock me. And they throw stuff onto the *Tia*'s deck sometimes. That's what she's called, the *Tia Maria*. I got some kind of turd in a Tupperware box last week."

"Jeez."

"There's a campaign going on, Joseph." George shook his head. "And that's why I'm worried, see. Because I've got to go away for a few days, and if they see that nobody's aboard I'm afraid they'll do something—sink her or burn her. So that's why I want somebody to sit out there while I'm away. And if your

15

Kelly's gone, then maybe you and me can do each other some good."

2

Truth is, George wanted me out on his *Tia Maria* right away. "The sooner I can get somebody, the sooner I'll be back," he said. "If you'll go out there tonight, I'll put three hundred bucks in your hand before I leave."

It all seemed a bit of a rush. But I'd already come close to getting into more woman trouble and the night was still young for that kind of thing. So I went back to the house, Kelly's and mine, and I packed up what I figured I'd need, like clothes and peanut butter.

And I wrote out a note for Kelly, in case she came back. I didn't want her to think I was at some woman's house. I told her I was being good because of my love for her and Little Joe. And I told her I was working and that I'd call home, because George promised there was a cell phone on the houseboat. But I didn't spell out where I was, because if she did come back, it would set her off again if she knew I was with George.

When I was done at home, I drove back to Berringers and met George and followed him in my truck out to the public launch ramp at the Geist Marina. There's a parking lot that was empty, but George had me park the truck on a side road nearby where it would be fine for three or four days and not get in anybody's way. I locked up and let him drive me down to the dock that's alongside the three-lane ramp for boats being driven up to be put in the lake. George had a dinghy tied up there. Even though it was only air-filled, it was big enough to have an outboard on the back.

I settled in while he revved the engine and then we were on our way. It was amazing how everywhere I looked on the shore there were houses and streetlights. I even saw a couple of houses where they had lakeside parties going on late and you could hear music. But at the same time it was also amazing how clear the stars were. Much clearer than ever in the city.

It was also cooler out on the lake than in the city. Cool and beautiful. For a time there I was really thinking about how I was doing the right thing.

The first I saw of the *Tia Maria* houseboat was when George pointed to some red lights ahead of us on the water. I wouldn't have noticed them for myself from the distance. "That's her," he said.

Only when we got up close, I found the boat wasn't what I was expecting at all. It looked like a raft with a big lean-to in the middle. "I thought a houseboat was long and thin," I said.

"Those are narrowboats," George said. "They're that way because they sail on rivers and canals."

"Oh."

"The *Tia* doesn't go anywhere. She just sits out here, anchored to the bottom. She doesn't look all that much, but she's very comfortable. Just like a lot of women."

I didn't say anything to that because women weren't what I wanted to think about.

A few minutes later, George tied the little boat up to the bigger one, and the whole thing was maybe twenty-five feet long and fifteen feet wide.

The first thing we did was head to one end where there was a boxed-in area. George opened up a door and took out a flashlight from a holder on the inside. That showed a motor. He primed it and pulled a cord and it started easily.

"Power," he said. He showed me three gas cans, and said there was plenty to provide electricity for three days, or a week if I turned the generator off when I didn't need it. Then we went inside.

Truth is, I liked what I saw when he turned the lights on. Whatever the "cabin" might look like from the outside, inside it was clean and well organized. There was a little TV, like he'd said. And a decent size bed once the couch was pulled out. Even a recliner.

"The kitchen is pretty basic," he said, when he showed me a sink in a corner. "The water from the faucet is from the lake. You want to drink water, use the bottled. But . . ." He opened a door. "You could always drink beer." The whole cupboard was stocked with six-packs. "The fridge isn't big, but it cools down fast when the power's on." And he showed me around the rest of the place: the toilet, the microwave, a gas ring. And a little shower. "But I hardly use it," he said. "We're surrounded by fucking water. I just jump in."

"George," I said, "did you build all this?"

He laughed. "You remember Morg?"

"Morg White?"

"Yeah."

Morgan White was one of our high school gang of six. He was the first one to go to jail, a juvie detention center, for throwing a brick at a bouncer at the Vogue when we all tried to get in there under-age. "He built this?"

"In his backyard. He had it in mind for a lake in Michigan where his father lived, but then his father died."

"He didn't want it for himself?" I hadn't seen Morg for years.

George shrugged. "He's in Terre Haute now. I took it off his wife's hands."

Terre Haute's a federal pen. "Oh."

"And that's about it. Anything else you want to know, or

want me to go over?"

"You said there's a phone."

"Oh. Right. Yeah, a cell phone." He showed me where it was on a shelf next to the couch-bed in a charger shaped like a high-heeled shoe.

There was only one person I had in mind to call, though I wasn't about to call her at her witch of a mom's apartment. But she might leave a message on my voicemail. And I could even change the outgoing message to include the phone number here in case she wanted to call and say, "Joe, I miss you so much . . ."

George was saying, "Well, I'm off now."

"Yeah?"

"I'll be back in three days. Four at the most."

"Aren't you forgetting something?"

He thought. "You're right. Come over here." He went to a closet we hadn't looked in and opened the door. There was a shotgun strapped to the back wall and boxes of shells on the floor. He unhooked the straps and took it out. "She's sweet," he said. "Pump action. But she's loaded, Joe. I should have remembered to tell you that. Don't want any nasty accidents." He pointed it at me and opened his eyes wide.

"Put it away, George."

He laughed, but he strapped it up again.

"Why have you got a shotgun out here?"

"Self-defense. And who knows? If some of the thugs on the lake get nasty, you might want it after all."

"To throw at them, you mean? Cause I've never shot a man yet and I'm not about to start now to defend some damn boat."

"Well, you know where it's at."

"I don't want no damn shotgun, George. What I want is the money you promised me. Cash, up front."

He pulled a roll of bills out of his pocket. He peeled off three hundreds and gave them to me. "Happy?"

"Yeah," I said. But I would of been happier if he'd kept on peeling till I had the whole two thousand to give back to Kelly.

"One last thing before I go," George said. He went to a drawer and pulled out a navy blue baseball cap. It had flip-down sunglasses and a white circle with an anchor in it on the front. "Got it just for you, Captain. Once I leave, you're in charge of this noble vessel and all who sail in her."

"So, I can marry people?"

"And bury them at sea. And make them walk the plank. As far as I'm concerned."

When I put the hat on he saluted me, then headed back outside.

I followed and watched him get into the inflatable outboard. "Hey, hang on a minute, George."

"What?"

"You're taking the boat?"

"Well, yeah."

"It's just . . . Well, what if something happens out here."

"Like what?"

"Like it sinks."

" 'She' Joe, not 'it.' Ships are always female. I'd have thought that a guy like you would know that instinctively."

"If she sinks."

"She won't." He pulled the cord to start the outboard.

"Or if some of these people who don't want you out here show up."

"Just stay on deck. Let them know she's occupied. They won't have the nerve do to anything with someone aboard. I mean, that is the point of your being out here."

"But I don't have any way to get off if something happens. A fire or something."

"You can swim, can't you, Joe?" George untied the little boat and the last thing I heard as he putted away was him chuckling.

3

I was not happy about being left with no way to get off the damn boat. George never even showed me a life jacket. I would of called him right then to ask, only he hadn't left me a number in case of emergency. It's not that I can't swim. I suppose I can. I just haven't had to do it for a long, long time. I even shouted after him, but there was no way he'd hear me over the outboard.

I was real antsy then, for a good hour. I wanted Kelly so bad. I couldn't remember ever wanting her more. Kelly, or somebody.

I couldn't stay still. I couldn't stay in the cabin, but when I went outside all I did was walk round and round. It was me who was walking the planks, all of them. I felt trapped, caged, panicky. I couldn't believe I'd gotten myself into this. I couldn't believe I let George talk me into something again, after all these years, after all the hard lessons. I never pretended to be any good at classroom-school, but I always figured I learned pretty good from life-school. Yet here I was. No place to go. No way to get a little warmth, a little distraction, a little affection.

I didn't know what to do. If I jumped into the lake and tried to swim, truth is, I'd probably drown. Truth is, I'm not much of a swimmer, never was. When the gang of us would go to a pool, or even out here to Geist, I never went in it.

For a few minutes I even thought about going to the closet and getting the shotgun and sticking it in my mouth. That's how far gone I felt.

But I didn't get the shotgun. I kept walking. And then I did some singing to myself, and eventually I calmed down enough to go inside and get a few beers and turn the TV on. The reception on it wasn't always good, but at least it was company, and after a while I pulled the bed out and later I fell asleep.

I woke up sweating, but it wasn't from nerves. The sun was shining right on my face.

The clock said it was about seven-thirty. That's later than the usual time Kelly and I wake up, but not later than we usually get up. Unless Little Joe is screaming or something. We stay in bed, me and Kelly. We cuddle and hug and stuff. Truth is, I love our mornings about more than anything.

But I was not with Kelly. Or with anybody else. I was on a pull-out couch in the middle of a fucking lake. I was here all day and at least two more to come and there was nowhere to go.

How did that happen?

But I remembered, clear enough. And there was nothing I could do about it, so I got up, went to the can, and set about making myself breakfast.

While I was boiling some water, I looked out the window and saw that at the front of the boat there was a deck chair and a little table.

The sun was bright and the day was beautiful, not hot yet, just real comfortable. And I figured I might as well eat outside. When I finished making breakfast, I found a tray and put the stuff on it. And then I put on my Captain's cap. If I was going to be in charge of this damn boat, I was going to wear my badge of office. I checked myself out in the mirror in the bathroom. Not bad.

I saluted myself. Permission to eat, please, sir?

I saluted myself back. Permission granted.

★　★　★　★　★

The lake and the food kept me calm so I could watch the boats that were round and about on the water. First there were fishermen, though they tended to keep near the shores. Then there were a couple of sailboats, and one little cabin cruiser.

And as I sat and watched, I realized there was a good side to all of this. There was no pressure on me to be anywhere on time or carry heavy stuff. And I was getting paid for it. Things could be worse. All I needed to make it good was Kelly.

Maybe sometime, when Kelly and me were back together again, maybe then me and her and Little Joe could come out here for a few days, or a week or something. Maybe George would want to go away for a few days and he'd hire me to boat-sit again. I could make it into a family vacation.

There wasn't much furniture on the houseboat, especially not for visitors, but we could bring folding chairs and picnic stuff. It was all a nice thing to think about. We'd need to have the dinghy, of course, because I know for a fact Kelly can't swim, any more than Little Joe can. And of course, I wouldn't be able to tell Kelly that the place was George's, but even so maybe it could all work out.

I got so excited thinking about it that I got up and went in. What I wanted to do was to call home and see if there were any messages from Kelly on my voicemail. She might even of asked me to call her back, knowing that her witch of a mother was out shopping or something.

But when I picked up the phone off its high-heeled shoe I couldn't make it work. I pushed all the buttons, over and over, but the little blank screen stayed blank. I was so frustrated I even shouted at it, and threatened it, and banged it on the wall, but nothing worked.

Finally I put it back and started looking through the drawers for an instruction book. But no matter where I looked, I couldn't find one. There were drawers and cupboards all over the place, but it was all George's clothes and condoms and old papers, and tools and bits of metal, and field glasses and tape cassettes and everything you could think of except instructions for the damn phone.

I just stood there shaking my head, because I felt even more cut off from Kelly than ever. I couldn't get any message she might of left me. I couldn't leave her a message of what my phone number here was, if she wanted to call me. Like if Little Joe got sick or she missed me real bad, or something.

I pounded the back of the recliner. I pounded on the little table. And then I thought about how if I smashed the table up into pieces of wood maybe it would float enough to help me if I tried to swim for shore.

It would serve George right if I did that. After all the times he'd screwed me, I owed him one by taking his money but not doing what he wanted.

Only truth is, I didn't want to break the table up and use it to help me swim to shore. I just wanted the phone to work.

Eventually, though, I calmed down some. Then I looked through the storage places again. I still didn't find the phone instructions, but this time I did find a little radio. It was like a prize possession or winning the lotto again. I carried it back out to the deck chair and turned it on. I found a "goldies" station—golden oldies—I like when I'm on the road and have a job with my truck.

Somehow that made it easier for me not to pick up messages from my voicemail, even if there were any. I was only here for a couple more days. And I did leave a note behind, in case Kelly came home. She was more likely to do that than call anyway since her witch of a mom would hardly ever go out and leave her alone.

Then I went and got a beer. I was being paid to boat-sit so I'd sit. Maybe later I'd look at the tools and bits and see if I could use some of them to fix the phone.

Meanwhile the cold beer was good. And it was nice to be able to drink it and not to think about if I was going to be driving later or not.

Funny, what I did think about was wondering how George got his mail out here. Wind and snow and rain was one thing, but I never heard of the US mail making lake deliveries. I didn't know why I thought of that. Maybe because my Uncle Al was a mailman and he used to be nice to me.

Later a motorboat came close enough for the noise of the motor to wake me up. That saved me a lot of grief because otherwise I'd of sunburned to a crisp out there. The boat was called the *Sunbird* and it had a kid and his girlfriend—not some angry, rich guy with any Tupperware or a blowtorch.

It's not that I burn easy. I spend time outdoors, and I'm dark enough naturally for it not to be a problem much. Kelly's the one with delicate skin. She said once that she could burn from the light in the refrigerator if she kept the door open too long.

The kid in the *Sunbird* and his girlfriend turned around after they went past and then came back a second time. This time they threw a bottle in the lake my way. It was nowhere close to the *Tia Maria* and it sank right away, but I waved a finger at them like they were naughty, naughty children. The girlfriend laughed, though the kid didn't even smile.

And then they went away. I went inside and looked in the bathroom and I found some sun-blocker in the cabinet. I didn't go right back outside again, though. I got another beer and turned the TV on.

Truth is, the kids in the *Sunbird* were the most exciting thing that happened during the whole day. It's not like the boy and his girlfriend were the only people out on the lake, but nobody else came close enough for me even to read the name on their boats.

I kept an eye out, in case of trouble, even when I was inside through the windows. But truth is, all there was for me to do was to watch TV, and drink beer, and go out on deck and listen to the radio and eat or look at stuff. Tough life, huh? When I think about how many times I've nearly busted a gut for a whole lot less than the three hundred I already had in my pocket, I could nearly laugh out loud.

Now and then in that first day it occurred to me maybe I ought to jump in the water to practice my swimming. It wasn't that I really thought I was ever going to have to swim for it, but you never know. I didn't know that I was going to be a boat-sitter, did I? And swimming laps around the boat would make me happier about being in the water if I ever needed it.

But in the end I just didn't feel like it. What I did instead was a long workout—push-ups and crunches and squats and so on. I figured that way if something bad did happen and I did have to swim for it, at least my muscles would be ready.

After the workout I thought again about jumping in the lake, just to cool off and get clean, but I took a shower instead. The water there was straight from the lake, so it was the same thing, really.

And later there was a ballgame on TV—the Cubs against the White Sox—which you used to never get to see before the inter-league games. So I cracked a few beers during that.

And after that I looked around some more and found some home-repair magazines, and more tools and some cleaning stuff. No instructions for the phone, though. And no life jacket.

The evening time was about the best. Once the sun went down

behind the hills in the west, lights started to go on in houses all over the shore even though it was still light in the sky. I got out George's field glasses and looked along the shore from through the windows inside the cabin. It would have been clearer to see from outside, but I wouldn't want anybody to see me with them and think I was spying on them. All I was doing was looking, not spying. And even from inside I was impressed how strong George's field glasses were.

I could see people outside their houses barbecuing food and playing catch. I could see into some of the rooms that faced my way, especially the picture windows. I enjoyed all that. It felt good to watch them go about their daily lives. It might be as close to how rich people live as I'd ever get.

If me and Kelly and Little Joe ever did come out here for a vacation then maybe Little Joe would want to use George's field glasses to make a fire from the sun, or burn up ants or something. I used to do that stuff with a magnifying glass I got out of a Cracker Jacks. Field glasses aren't much different from a Cracker Jacks magnifying glass. It's all a lens.

Later on I made a couple of peanut butter sandwiches for dinner because I wasn't feeling like cooking anything fancy in the microwave. And I began to wish again about the phone so I could pick up messages on my voicemail from Kelly, if she left any.

Truth is, I got edgier again the more into the evening it went on. Maybe it's something to do with it getting dark. If I'd of been at home I'd of been down at Berringers for sure. So in a way it was a good thing I was stuck out here instead.

So I had some beers and watched the TV. It would of been better if George had cable or satellite or something. There was a VCR, but I didn't find any tapes anyplace I looked so far. Maybe I'd talk to him about all that beforehand if me and Kelly and

Little Joe ever set it up to come out here. I could make it all a condition, and say I wouldn't house-sit again without it.

I got so bad about half past nine that I took off everything but my shorts and I lowered myself into the water by the boat. It was to cool me off, in more ways than one. But what was in the back of my mind was that if it felt right maybe I could swim for shore and walk to a bar and be sociable with other people for a while. I wasn't planning to go into the bar in only my shorts, but going into the water was a test. If it felt OK I'd work the rest of it out later.

Unfortunately, it didn't feel right at all. The water was warm enough. It was fine. But I wasn't fine. As soon as I was in up to my neck my heart started racing and I breathed real hard, like my lungs thought each time would be the last. I got back out almost as soon as I got in.

Even so, I did feel more relaxed once I got out of the water and calmed down some. So I had another beer and watched more TV from the bed. A good moment was when I remembered to pull a curtain over the little window the sun woke me up through the day before.

Even so, I was up before the sun on the second day. That whole second day was hard. I mean hard. I was antsy almost nonstop. I must of done five full sets of workouts, just to keep from going crazy. I ran around the deck more times than I remembered to count.

It's not like anything different happened from the first day. Maybe that was the problem. I got to the point in the second day where I was thinking about jumping up and down and calling to some of the passing boats to come and rescue me. Maybe if one had got close enough I would of.

★ ★ ★ ★ ★

But it was the third day that was the killer.

For a start I slept badly. I kept hearing noises in the night like people were trying to get on board. Each time I got up, nobody was there, but then it would all happen again. I even thought about getting out the shotgun to keep by my bed. I wasn't about to use it to defend any houseboat, but there was also me to defend.

But truth is, nothing happened in the whole night. No raiders, no firebombs, no Tupperware.

What happened was in the middle of the morning.

I was sitting out in the deck chair with the radio and a beer trying to feel calm because probably it was my last day. And I was looking at the houses on the eastern shore through the field glasses. What I saw was a dirty white truck pull up at the side of a big house and park. Because of trees and stuff I couldn't see this truck clearly, but even so from the minute I spotted it what came into my mind was that it looked like my truck.

There was no way it could be my truck, of course. My truck was locked up near the marina, and I had the keys. But on the other hand a truck, one you've had for years, one you could only afford to buy new because you had a win on the lotto, well, you know a truck like that when you see it. And the more I looked at what I could see of the truck by the house, the more I would of sworn it was mine.

But there was no way to check. All I could do was watch. And what I saw was a couple of guys go into the house and bring bags out to load up. And I couldn't see the guys clearly either. They had overalls and hats on, and there were bushes and trees in their way too, no matter how strong the field glasses were.

I wanted to see better so bad that I even thought about cutting the *Tia Maria*'s anchor ropes. If I'd been sure the boat would float to a place that would help, I might of done it. But after about half an hour the two guys got back in the truck and drove away again.

And then damned if I didn't see the truck again. It pulled up behind another house, only about four along from the first one, though farther away from where I could see. But it was the same two guys in hats and they were loading stuff in the truck that came from the house again.

What the hell was going on? Was I crazy? Was it even my truck? But at the moment I saw her the second time I knew in my heart, even more than before, that it was my truck, even though it couldn't be.

After the two guys drove away from this second house I looked and looked to see if they went to another house, but I never saw them again. I just sat there, going over and over everything that happened. And one of the things I went over was when George found me in Berringers. What he said when he tapped me on the shoulder was that he'd been hoping he'd run into me that night. Well, what if he was looking for me because he knows I have a truck? And what if he only spun me this yarn about his boat being in danger so I'd sit out in the middle of the lake while he could use my truck himself without having to ask? Locks on a truck mean nothing to a guy like George. As kids we could all get into locked vehicles so fast that we raced each other sometimes for the hell of it. After a while we had keys that would work in a lot of the cars too, though I never kept mine.

And maybe the idea of it all came from George sitting out here on the houseboat with the field glasses just like I was doing. Maybe while he watched the rich houses on the shore he got to know that a bunch of them were empty now, like for summer vacations. Like they loaded up the car, or a taxi came. And maybe he figured all he needed was a truck to go and rob them. And, if he was using my truck, then if anybody noticed or took the license number they would find that the truck was owned by me, who had a record. And when the cops came to me, I wouldn't have an alibi because nobody I knew had seen me for three days.

I got real edgy then. I got up and walked around and around. The last place I wanted to go was to prison. I was lucky not to go there the last time, and how could I ever explain it this time to Kelly, especially since here I was involved with goddamn George Wayne again. I'd lose Kelly for sure, if I hadn't lost her already.

What I did was change into underpants that look a lot like training shorts and put my wallet and keys in a plastic bag. What I had in mind was to swim for the shore and walk back to where my truck ought to be when I left it. If it was there, and I was wrong about George using it, never mind and to hell with him. I'd still just drive it home. And if it wasn't there, then the money I had would be enough to get me home anyway. At least that way I could talk to someone that knew me and get my alibi back. I'd sort the rest of everything out with George later, which was maybe just as well because I was so mad at him right now.

So I jumped into the lake with my plastic bag and I managed to paddle a few yards in the direction of the land, but then I got real nervous about drowning so I turned around. For one thing I'd had quite a few beers already, and you're not supposed to swim after eating, I knew that much. So I crawled back up onto the *Tia Maria* and decided to try to think of another plan.

If only there was a phone I could work, then I could call 911. That way the cops might catch George and the guy who was helping him in the act. It's not natural for me to talk to cops by volunteering but I still went back inside to try the phone again. Sometimes machines like phones do seem to heal themselves.

Not this time, though. I still couldn't get the phone to turn on. Then I thought maybe it was just something simple like a loose wire inside that I would see if I opened it up. So I took one of George's screwdrivers and what I found was a loose wire all right—the one that connected to where a battery ought to of been.

George might of forgotten to put one in. But maybe he took it out on purpose so I wouldn't be able to call 911 if I saw my truck robbing houses on the shore. And that's what I'd of bet on, for sure. If George had walked in that minute, I'd of put the phone where he could never use it, and its high-heel cradle, too.

I was so mad I knew it was important for me to try to calm down. So I took a few more beers out to the deck again and sat in the sun and tried to think of what else I could do.

Then after a while, the *Sunbird* motorboat that woke me up the first day and saved me from sunburn came by. I saw that it was the same kid and the same girl in it—they were still the only people who ever got close enough to the *Tia Maria* for me to recognize.

They went past laughing and then they turned around to come back again. And I got an idea.

I jumped up and called to them, "Hey, help! Help me!"

The boy slowed the motorboat down as it got closer and I called again, "Hey, *Sunbird*, my name's Joe. Please, I need to get ashore." I held up one of the beers and my wallet. "I can give you beer, or money. At least come close where we can talk about it."

I could tell the boy was thinking about it, though he never turned the motor off. And if they would give me a ride back to the marina or wherever they came from, then I could walk to where my truck was supposed to be and find out fast if it was there or not. And I wouldn't be out in the middle of a damn lake.

I saw the boy and the girl talk to each other a minute, and

the girl was looking at me while the boy talked to her. Even from the distance, I thought I recognized the look she was giving. And maybe I was right about that because all of a sudden the damn boy speeded up his boat again and my chance to get back on dry land was over.

I was pissed off about it at first, but after I had another beer I realized that at least now I could have an alibi. I knew the *Sunbird* name and I was sure that the girl would recognize me again if we had a lineup. At least she would if I was stripped down to my shorts.

And after that the day was easier again for a while. I watched some television and even fell asleep to it in the afternoon. By nighttime I decided to make a real meal and I cooked up some potatoes and hotdogs in the microwave, and later on I microwaved some popcorn I found, too.

I only got edgy again when I started to think about what I should say to George when he got back. One of the problems with that was I didn't know when he'd come back. He said "three or four" days. It'd been three already. So he had to be back by tomorrow.

Only what if he wasn't? Before that minute it never crossed my mind that George might not come back at all and just leave me out here. He had stuff here, sure, but not much that was valuable except maybe the field glasses. The TV wasn't a fancy one, and as for the phone . . .

Thinking all that got me real edgy again, but this time it wasn't because I wanted some company. I was edgy because I hated damn George Wayne so much for making a fool of me. I don't like it from anybody, but from George it's extra worse because of the history.

It was about then that I got out the shotgun and looked it over and made sure that I understood how it worked. That sounds a bit dumb, maybe, because it's a gun and it has a trigger so what's to understand? But some guns have safety catches and even with this one you had to pump it to change a cartridge.

I didn't shoot it off—though I thought about it, just popping away out onto the lake where there wasn't anybody. But it was about dark and I couldn't see very well so I couldn't be sure nobody was there. I wouldn't want to kill someone. Not a stranger.

I began to think about killing George, though.

I'm not a natural killer, but if all this that he'd done was going to cost me Kelly and Little Joe forever, then he deserved whatever he got.

I began to think that maybe the best way would be to catch him by surprise as he came back. If I listened, I'd be able to hear him coming from a long way and get ready. I could catch him when he was on the edge of the houseboat. That way he'd just fall into the lake and be gone. The water looked deep. I could throw the shotgun in after him.

I'd have to make sure not to hit the dinghy, though. It was air-filled. If I hit the dinghy then I'd have no way to get back to my truck. So maybe I should just shoot over his head first, to show him who was boss. Then I could make him tell me the whole truth before I blew him away. He did say I could make people walk the plank as far as he was concerned. When I remembered that I smiled. I've never killed a man before, but truth is, the thought of killing George made me feel better.

Though it would be just like him not to come back to the houseboat at all and screw up my plans. I swore to myself that I would never, ever, get involved in anything of any kind with George Wayne again, even if he had a fist full of hundred-dollar bills and all he wanted me to do was take them.

Then that reminded me of the roll of bills he was carrying. I didn't like the idea of being a thief, but on the other hand,

George owed me two grand. Or at least he owed Kelly. She'd be impressed if I could give her that back at last.

And I really hoped I'd get my truck back. We'd been together so long.

Damn George.

And then I began to think more seriously about what I should do if he did never come back . . .

What I thought about was if there was any way I could get myself to the shore without George's dinghy. I was worried about drowning, but if I had something to hang onto, like a raft . . .

I got out some of George's tools and looked around for pieces of wood that I could nail together. There wasn't much loose wood, so I took a deep breath and whacked off the top of the table by the recliner. That felt good. Like I'd done it to George's head.

I pulled doors off the cupboards then, and took out a bunch of drawers and dumped what was in them on the floor, and before long I had something that would be big enough for me to put all my stuff on and it would still float.

The plan was to have it float in the water and I would hang on the edge and kick my feet and not feel like I was going to go under any minute. Even if it took a long time, I still ought to be able to get to the shore that way with all my things.

The more I thought about my plan, the better I liked it. I even got some more ideas. I took the box of George's condoms that I found and blew a bunch of them up. When I had six blown up I tied them to places on the raft.

Then I took another condom and worked my wallet into it, which was helped by the lubrication. With my wallet in, I put my truck keys in too, and then I tied the end and fitted it all so I'd have it all hanging from my neck. That way I'd have a hand free to help my feet swim with and I'd go faster. And, no matter what happened, I'd still have keys to the truck and the three hundred dollars to give to Kelly.

The next thing I did was test how the raft floated. I carried it all to the edge and eased it over. And I was happy as I could be when it just sat there in the water like a raft with the condom-balloons not even low enough to be needed to help the floating. I tied it to the *Tia* with some of the same string I'd been using for everything and I went back inside to pack up my clothes. I put them all in a plastic bag—everything but my training shorts/underpants—and took them back out to the raft.

What I didn't like was how much the weight of my clothes and stuff seemed to sink the raft. So I took the bag off and decided to leave some things behind, like my peanut butter. The lighter load did make a difference.

I couldn't think of anything else to do, so I slid into the water beside my raft, and worked my way round to where it was closest to the eastern shore, and then I pushed off.

4

I kept telling myself it was like walking on the edge of a tall building. I kept saying, Look at the lights on the shore. Don't look down.

Truth is, it was scary as hell and about drove me crazy.

I kept paddling and paddling with my feet and my free arm, only it felt like I never got anywhere, and the lights looked the same all the time and no closer. There was some wind against me, and sometimes I felt things around my feet that I didn't understand, like a current.

I got real antsy.

I wanted to turn around and go back. It couldn't be far. But over and over I wouldn't let myself do it.

Until I couldn't take it anymore and finally I did look around for where the houseboat was.

Only I couldn't see it anymore. But the twist of turning to look back made the raft wobble. I had no idea wood rafts on the water were so unstable, even with balloon-condoms to help them.

What a crazy idea all this was. I was out in the middle of a fucking lake in my underpants and truth is, I couldn't swim worth a damn. I knew—knew—I was going to die, and all I had to show for my life was Little Joe, and now I wasn't going to be able to see him grow up and tell him the things a father ought to tell his son.

Then something nibbled my toe. I screamed. I really did, and

I jerked my foot right up and if I didn't know better I'd of thought I jerked it right out of the water and over my head.

I turned to look for the houseboat again. It didn't matter anymore what George Wayne did to me, or to my truck, even if he ended me in jail. Being alive still had to be better than being pulled under by my feet down into the depths of the lake and worth the price.

Only I couldn't find where the houseboat was anymore. It had to be there.

Something nibbled my toe again. I pulled my knees up near my chest, even though I nearly sank to my chin.

Didn't I leave the lights on that showed where the houseboat was?

I must of left some lights on, because I never turned any off.

And then I saw a light that I figured might be it because there wasn't a choice of any other. Only it was in a different direction than just straight back, and very far away.

Something nibbled my toe even pulled up like it was. I had to twist hard to get my foot away from it. I thrashed around, a really big thrash that I thought was sure to scare it away, whatever it was.

At least I got my toe free. Which was a relief, though I kept my feet up anyway.

But then, I didn't have my raft anymore. Where was it? My raft! All my clothes. It was gone. Gone! I couldn't see it anywhere.

I'd never for a minute thought I might lose it. If I thought ahead, I could of put a flashlight on it, or something to tie it to me.

But I didn't.

And without the raft to hold onto I felt myself sinking. For a minute I thought it was all over, I really did.

And then my toe touched something.

I jerked my legs up again and thrashed my arms, only this time I was trying to get myself toward the lights of shore.

And a minute later I finally realized what my toe had been feeling, because my other toe felt it too. It was seaweed. Or lakeweed. Whatever—a growing kind of stuff. Because in a minute both my feet hit the ground, and instead of drowning I was standing.

The lights of the houses were still far away, but only because they were set back from the shore. In fact I was able to walk to dry land and drag myself onto dirt, and then grass.

I was ashore. I had my wallet and keys. I'd made it.

I just lay on that precious grass, for longer than I could remember. I was exhausted. Every muscle in my arms and legs and body cried out.

After a while, though, I remembered that this was only the first step of what I had to do. Where my truck ought to be was north of here, near the marina. I knew which way to go but not how far.

It was also a problem that all I had on was underpants, though I did still have my keys and also my driver's license. A good thing was it was a warm night.

And then I heard something moving in bushes near to where I was lying. I stayed very still, even though I wasn't going anywhere at the time already. The last thing I needed was a wild animal.

And I heard breathing. And it wasn't my own.

I looked up then and what I saw was the face of a little dog right in my face. I would of jumped back in surprise if I wasn't lying down.

The dog just looked at me. It was white and from what I could see it was like a tiny poodle. "Hi, doggie," I said.

It tilted its head.

"Nice doggie."

And then it started to bark. They were little yapping barks but very loud.

At first I thought it would stop. When it didn't, I didn't know what to do, so I got up.

Behind the dog, a long way from us, a light went on. I could see a man in a doorway. And I realized I needed to decide if I was going to go up to the house for help. Or run.

A woman joined the man in the doorway. Then the man pulled out what looked like a baseball bat and opened the door. That kind of decided it for me.

The mini dog only followed me for a little way before it stayed behind and stopped barking. Truth is, I was glad it didn't run with me, because I might of stepped on it and squashed it to death.

Once I got away and into some trees I stopped to listen for whether anybody was following, but I didn't hear anyone. What I did then was turn to head inland between some houses.

I could of followed the shore, but that was bound to be not nearly so much of a straight line as a road. My idea was to look like I was a guy in a swimming suit out for a walk.

I found the road at the front of the houses easily enough and began walking. I got caught stepping on some pebbles before I began to look out for them where there were streetlights. At least I knew I was making progress toward where my truck ought to be as long as I kept the lake on my left.

To begin with whenever cars passed by, I tried to find some shadows. But then I wondered if that made me look like a burglar. And besides, I wasn't doing anything wrong. They might even give me a lift. So I thumbed the next car and the car after that, but they didn't stop.

After what felt like an hour of walking a car did stop for me.

A police car.

I didn't see it coming up behind. Probably I would of ducked out of the way. Or run.

But as soon as I saw it, they turned their spotlight on me and through a loud speaker a guy said, "Police. Stop right there."

All I could do was stop.

The light was so bright it blinded me, but I heard a door that I guessed must be a cop getting out, and then I saw him coming around the front to where I was standing. "Whatcha doing here, buddy?" he asked, but I could see his face now and that he was surprised by looking up close that all I had on was underpants.

"I'm walking up to the marina."

He turned to the car and shaded his eyes. "Kill the spot, Janine, and come and look at this."

The light went out and by the time I could see again after adjusting my eyes, there were two cops and one of them was a woman one. She said, "Where are your clothes, pal?"

"On a raft on the lake."

"Where?"

The man cop laughed. "You going to frisk him?"

"It's a long story," I said, "but where I'm going now is up to the marina because that's where my truck ought to be, if it's still there."

"Go on, Jan," the man cop said. "Frisk him."

"You got any ID?" the woman asked.

"Yeah." My wallet and keys were still in the condom around my neck.

"Is that what I think it is?" the woman asked as I peeled the condom back and took out my wallet.

"I bet I know what's going on," the man cop said suddenly. "It's a stag night, right? You're on your stag night and your buddies left you out in the middle of nowhere in your underwear."

It was the woman laughing now, but at the same time she took my wallet to see my driver's license. "Joseph Prince. That you?"

"Yes, ma'am."

"You're not from this part of town, are you, Joe?"

"I live on the southside, near Fountain Square."

"I remember a stag night I was on," the man cop said. "It was the cousin of one of my high school buddies, and we took that poor sap all the way to Hardscrabble. You know? Out west on 36. And all we left him was three pieces of cardboard with the letters 'S,' 'E,' and 'X' on them—like Scrabble letters, you know? So you're lucky you still got your underpants, Joe."

"I thought stag nights were about strippers," the woman cop said.

"Some are, some aren't."

"I'm going to have them run Joseph Prince through the computer," the woman said. "You got any outstanding warrants, Joe?"

"No, ma'am."

"It's the women that have the strippers nowadays," the man cop said. "Things just ain't what they used to be."

The woman cop was about back in the car when the man said to me, "So, what's she like, your gal, Joe? Pretty?"

"Very pretty," I said.

"Big knockers? Good in the sack?"

I didn't want to say anything about Kelly that way, so I didn't.

"I bet she is." The man cop sighed. "I bet she is."

We stood there a quiet minute before the woman cop called out, "He's clean."

"You heard the lady, Joseph," the man cop said. He took a step toward the car and then stopped. "Word of advice, buddy."

"Yeah?"

"Enjoy marriage while you can." He gave his head a quick

shake, and went back to the car.

When the light went on from him opening the door I could see the woman cop had something to say to him. Then after a minute she got out on her side and said, "We don't want you wandering our streets, Joe. We're going to take you to the marina."

And that was just fine with me. I wasn't wet anymore, but my feet sure were tired of walking barefoot.

They let me out where I asked, which was in the parking lot near the public launch ramp. "I don't see a truck," the woman cop said.

"It'll be close by."

"You sure?"

I rattled my keys. "I'll be fine. Thanks a lot."

"OK, Joe. Good luck." She waved and pulled off. The man cop hadn't said anything more for the whole ride.

I waved back until they were gone and truth is, I was glad to be out of their car because of the air-conditioning. They needed it, I guess, but that was because they had clothes.

When they were out of sight I headed for the side road where I left my truck in the first place. I didn't have a watch anymore, but you could tell it was late by how many cars weren't on the streets and how many lights weren't on in houses. Even so, I wasn't tired myself. I was excited, because maybe I was finally going to get my truck back. And go home.

Maybe I'd even find Kelly and Little Joe there. Maybe they came back and got the note I left and couldn't wait to see me again like I wanted to see them. That would be good. So gooood.

Only my truck was not where I left it.

I must of stood and looked at the space for five whole minutes. I thought through everything I remembered to make sure that this had to be the place. And it was. I was sure.

Even so, I walked around all the blocks nearby in case there was another road that looked the same. And then I went back to the parking lot and started over. But each time I came to the same place. Where my truck was gone.

So it was true. George did take it while he left me stuck out on his damn houseboat. I could of killed him then.

There was a little hill up from the road where the truck wasn't. Somebody's yard that led to bushes and a tree. I climbed up to where I wouldn't be seen from the road so I could figure out what to do now. I just hoped there was no tiny poodle here.

So George was robbing houses with my truck . . . Damn George.

At least I had my alibi back with the two cops, if he was still doing it tonight. What I didn't have back was a way to get home.

If it wasn't so late, I could of found a public phone and called a taxi. But all I had was paper money, so I couldn't use a phone until I found someplace open to give me change, a store or gas station.

I tried to remember if I saw any while I was riding with the cops. Only I didn't.

At least I was lucky it was such a warm night. Even just in my underpants I wasn't cold at all. And it did feel good to sit on the grass. I lay down on it and looked up at the sky between the branches. I wasn't on the lake anymore, but I could still see lots more stars than I ever could in the city. Lots more.

And then, after a while, I heard something.

It was a motor in the distance. I couldn't tell what kind at first. And then I recognized it. It was the sound of a little outboard motor. Could it be George, coming back to his boat?

That seemed crazy, because how could I hear it where I was now?

Even so, I looked all around and finally I saw what it really was. It wasn't an outboard motor at all. It was a little motor scooter.

And it also wasn't George. It was a girl. The girl from the *Sunbird* boat. I don't know how she found me here, but it made me remember how I recognized that look on her face.

She stopped her scooter in the same space where my truck ought to be. I sat up and waved to her and she waved back. She was smiling and I saw she was pretty with long blonde hair and a bikini on. She got off her scooter and took something from the box on the back. It was a coil of rope. She threw it up to me and said, "Catch."

I caught it but I didn't know what to do then.

"You going to help me up the hill?"

I pulled on the rope and she held on and came up to where I was. When she got close she reached out her hand and I took it. It was soft and warm and I suddenly felt good because I was touching another human being and I was going to have some company again. It seemed like forever since the last time.

But once she was standing next to me on the grass she pulled her hand back. "Are you the same guy I saw this afternoon?"

"Are you the same girl?"

"I sure am, Joe." And she started taking her bikini off.

And—I couldn't believe it—once she had her clothes off she was Kelly. She was Kelly all the time! She was fed up with her witch of a mother and found a motor scooter and she came all the way out here to see me. I was so happy.

"Oh Joe," she said.

"Oh baby," I said.

And then it was morning and I woke up with the sun streaming onto my face, like it did that first morning I woke up on the houseboat so hot and sweaty.

And even though being with Kelly turned out to be just a

dream I was still glad it was a new day because now I could get myself home at last, with a taxi, or maybe a bus.

Only when I walked down the hill to the road again, my truck was there.

Right where it was supposed to be. Right where I parked it in the first place.

I could hardly believe it. I walked all around it, to make sure it was really my truck. The only thing that was different was where somebody wrote "Adge" in the dirt on the hood.

When I tried the door it was locked like I left it. I used my key and opened it. It was my truck, all right. It was my stuff in the glove compartment and nothing missing.

I didn't get it.

Was it possible she was there all the time and somehow I didn't see her?

Or did George bring her back while I was asleep?

And yet I didn't really care. I had her back. And I could drive her home to where maybe Kelly was waiting with Little Joe. And even if they weren't, at least I'd be home again and it would all be over.

Only instead of starting her up, I didn't. I got out again and went to open the back. I was afraid of what I would find inside.

But when I opened her up, everything was the way it was supposed to be. I have blankets and ropes and tools I use for moving things, and they were all where I keep them. I couldn't see a single thing that was out of place.

I went back to the cab and looked around there more carefully and finally I found what made me sure I wasn't a completely froot-loop and crazy and that the truck had been gone and used and brought back. What I found was that on the floor and under the seats it had been swept out. Or maybe even vacuumed. What I found was that it was a lot cleaner than when I left it.

I didn't know George was so neat. Well, the houseboat was pretty tidy, except maybe inside his drawers.

Then I thought about how I whacked off the top of his table and emptied so many drawers onto the floor so I could use them for the wood. For a minute I had a pang because of the destruction. Especially now it turned out he came back in the night, and it was at the end of the third day, like he said it probably would be.

But to hell with George. And to hell with what I did to his stuff. He deserved whatever he got because he used my truck without permission.

Didn't he? I couldn't of seen the truck through the field glasses and then not seen it here when I looked last night. Could I?

Well, if George didn't like what I did, then let him come to the house and complain. Let him come with Kelly there. She'd give him something to remember, especially about the two grand he owed her.

She's strong, my Kelly, and not just in personality. She works at it because her plan is to become a personal trainer for people one day when Little Joe is old enough. And maybe one day she'll own her own gym, if she can ever get that two grand back, and more besides.

So let George complain to her and see how he makes out.

The truck started first time like she always does, and I drove her home.

When I got to the house, though, I found the note I left for Kelly right where I left it. She wasn't back, or Little Joe. That brought my heart right down, because I had hopes of finding her in our bed the way she ought to be this early in the morning.

But she wasn't. And there wasn't anything I could do about it.

So I lay down in our bed and I pretended Kelly was in the house but somewhere else, like maybe she only got up to go to the bathroom. And even though it was daytime, I slept.

And it was peaceful because at least all the stuff about George and the houseboat was over now at last.

Or so I thought.

5

What woke me up was the phone ringing. I grabbed for it and said, "Kelly?"

But it wasn't. It was a guy I was supposed to be moving furniture for this morning and already I was late. I didn't even have to check my work planner now that I remembered it. Though usually it's Kelly that keeps track of my work for me, when she's home.

All I could do was jump out of bed and put on my clothes and get over there as fast as I could.

And it turned out that for both of the next two days after I got home, I had a lot of work. It was more than just the furniture move I forgot. I got two more "soon as possible" jobs from people that called from the ads that I leave up on walls and mailboxes and windows all over town.

That's how I keep my business going. Whenever I don't have work on a day, I go out and put up posters saying no job too small for my big truck. You have to sow to reap, and all I have to sow with is my time and my posters. The posters have my number people can tear off. Sometimes while I watch TV I use the time to do the cutting between the numbers for my posters to make them easier to tear.

What was the biggest surprise to me was not the sudden burst of work, but that at the end of both days I was so tired that I just ate and went to sleep and didn't even feel like going to Berringers.

I only ever thought about women and their company in the mornings those days, or else at strange times like when I was driving from one place to another. I still got the feeling for company, really strong, and sometimes it would of been hard to keep away if I hadn't been in the middle of so much work to do. But the amazing part was that by the end of the day when I could of gone to Berringers I didn't really feel like it, so I didn't.

It made me believe that maybe I'd cracked it. Maybe during those damn days out on the lake, going cold turkey, maybe I had grown up about women at last. I sure hoped so. And I sure hoped that Kelly would understand it, even though in both those two days since I got back she never called when I was home nor left a message when I wasn't. Even still, by now I'd gone about a whole week—if you didn't count what I would of done with Melody, if George hadn't come into Berringers and broken it up.

What's more, I still had the three hundred bucks I'd earned off George, plus more from the jobs I was doing and some more yet that was owed. There's nothing I wanted so bad as to provide some good living for Kelly and Little Joe.

But then, then, just as things seemed to be looking up, then it all went crazy.

When it happened was in the night after the second day of work—the early morning of it. It was about three a.m., though I didn't stop to look at the clock.

I was asleep at the time, and there was a loud knocking on my door and voices shouting and before I could even think that it might be Kelly, only she has a key, suddenly my room was full of cops. They dragged me out of bed and pushed me onto the floor and handcuffed me behind my back and didn't even let me get dressed.

One cop stayed with me while the others went crashing

around our little house with guns out and calling, "Clear!" like they thought Little Joe was in the kitchen with a machine gun and was about to blow them all away to save his dad.

Finally they worked out there was nobody but me. The cop in charge was a woman. She wasn't in uniform like the others, but she was taller than them, and scary, with big curly hair and big shoulders. She said, "Sit him up."

A couple of the uniforms pulled me up.

The woman said, "Jesus Christ, get him some clothes. We don't want to stand here looking at that."

Because they didn't want to take the handcuffs off, it meant that one of the cops had to dress me. I maybe wouldn't of cooperated—since they weren't there from an invitation—but since it was a woman in charge I didn't kick up a fuss. There seemed to be enough fuss going on already.

They got me in my shorts and a pair of pants and that seemed to be enough for the scary woman cop. "So, Mr. Prince, what have you got to say to us?"

"What have I got to say to you? Are you crazy? You're the ones that broke in here. I've got a little boy. What if he'd been home? You'd of scared the shit out of him."

"Where is your little boy?" the woman cop asked. "You kill him, too?"

"What?"

"I asked if you killed your little boy."

"You're . . . You're not saying Little Joe is dead? Please to God, tell me he's not."

"I'm not telling you he's dead."

"And Kelly?"

"Who is Kelly?"

One of the other cops leaned toward her. She had to bend over for this guy to whisper in her ear, that's how big she was. "Kelly is your girlfriend, yeah?" she said then.

"She sure is. Is she all right?"

"You tell me, Mr. Prince."

I shook my head. "I haven't seen her for more than a week."

"Where is she?"

"With her mother."

"She left you?"

"Yeah."

"Why'd she leave you, Joe? Did you hit her? Did you threaten to kill her? Did she feel that she and the child were in danger?"

"Shut up!" I shouted. "Why are you saying all this talk about killing and threats? I would never ever ever hurt a hair on Kelly's head. She'll tell you that. And Little Joe? That's plum crazy."

"Would you hurt a hair on George Wayne's head, Joe?"

I was knocked back for a minute, cause I thought we were talking about Kelly and Little Joe. "What about George's head?"

"You don't deny knowing George Wayne?"

"Of course I know George. We went to high school."

"When did you see him last, Joe?"

I worked it out. "Six days ago. Well, six nights."

"You sure about that?"

"Yeah, I'm sure."

"You sure it wasn't last night, Joe?"

"It wasn't last night. Why are you asking? Has something happened to George?"

"What might happen to George?"

"I don't know, but the way you're talking . . ."

"He seem all right to you last night?"

She almost caught me there for a second, because I was picturing George when he left me on the houseboat in his dinghy. He seemed all right. "I didn't see him last night. It was six nights ago."

"Well, we don't think so, Joe. We think you saw him last night."

53

"I didn't."

It was then that one of the other cops showed the woman cop my wallet. She said, "More than four hundred dollars in here, Joe."

"And there better stay four hundred and thirty-six in there too," I said, because more than once friends of mine said the cops arresting them skimmed from the cash they were carrying.

"Where'd you get all this money?"

"By working for it. Where do you get yours?" I was pissed off with being put back to kneel on the floor in handcuffs with everybody standing around me and no shirt on. The least they could do was let me sit on the bed. I knew Kelly wasn't likely to come home at that time in the morning, but what if she did? She'd come in and think all kinds of bad things about me, and maybe turn round and never come back. I'd hate for that to happen about worse than anything.

"You sure you worked for it? Because I think you got it by emptying George Wayne's wallet after you shot him."

"George was shot? Jesus. Is he OK? I mean, is he going to be OK?"

"George Wayne is dead, Joe."

"Oh my God."

"Most of George Wayne's head was blown away by a shotgun, Joe. Somebody made a half-assed attempt to make it look like suicide, but it was murder."

"Murder?"

"But why am I telling you all this—you already knew."

"Are you crazy? How would I know that? Or was it on the radio?"

She laughed and made a smirk to one of the other cops. "He's good," she said. "I'll give him that."

I didn't get it until she turned back to me bent down so she could put her face right up close to mine. "How did you know?

Because you're the one who shot him, Joe."

"No I didn't." I tried to get up then, but one of the other cops pushed me down on the head so I stayed where I was.

"You pointed the shotgun at your high school buddy and pulled the trigger and blew his fucking brains all over the wall."

"I did not do any such a thing."

"I think you did kill George Wayne, Joe. Do you know why I think that?"

"Why?"

"Because your fingerprints are all over the goddamn shotgun, Joe."

Oh. "I . . . I can explain that."

"So can I."

"It's not from—"

"They're there because you forgot to wipe them off, you were in such a rush to get at Wayne's wallet."

"He . . . He didn't have a wallet. Well, maybe he did, but he kept his money in a roll in his pocket. I know because I saw it when he gave me my three hundred. He had a whole lot more in that roll. It looked like thousands."

The big woman cop didn't have anything to say to that for a minute and it was then that another of the cops leaned in to whisper to her. She turned away from him, kind of angry. "I already read him his rights, Dave. You heard me."

"No, you didn't," I said.

"Oh yeah, Sarge," the Dave cop said. "I remember now."

"You didn't," I said.

"But you know your rights, don't you, Joe?" the woman said to me.

"I guess. I get a phone call. And I can have a lawyer."

"See, Dave," the woman said. "He remembers. And you have the right to remain silent, Joe. But if you want my advice, you won't. If you want my advice you'll just tell me what happened—hey, things happen . . . I know that, you know that. But once you have a lawyer involved there's no way I can cut you any slack for cooperating or for mitigating circumstances."

"What slack?"

"Well, it depends what happened. Say, if it all started as self-defense, for instance. Maybe he came at you and then maybe you panicked and at the end you fought over the shotgun and it went off and you ran for it."

"I didn't do any of that."

"Or you could tell me where you hid the rest of George's money. Or maybe some other guy was out there on the boat. Maybe the other guy pulled the trigger and you tried to stop him. See, all those things, if you tell me now then maybe I can make this an easier ride for you." She waved to the two closest cops. "Dave, Scotty, get Joe here up off the floor so he can sit and talk to me and be more comfortable."

The two cops lifted me up and sat me on the bed. "That's better," the woman cop said. "See, in a situation like this, Joe, there's the easy way and the hard way. We can make this a whole lot easier for you—if you have the right attitude and we talk it all through, here and now. So what do you say, Joe? C'mon, tell me what happened out there on the houseboat. How'd it all begin?"

"What I say," I said, "is I want a lawyer."

"Oooo, not smart, Joe." The woman cop was frowning over me.

"I want a lawyer. A free one." I remembered from the last time how they would appoint a free lawyer to me. It wasn't because I'd need a lawyer for what I didn't do to George, though. What I figured was if I had a lawyer on my side from the start there was a better chance I'd get my same four hundred and thirty-six dollars back for Kelly when they finally let me go.

Once they were done looking around the house, they drove me downtown. I was in the back while the Dave cop drove and the big woman rode as passenger. They didn't talk to me because of correct procedure and I just sat there thinking what a dumb mess it all was.

Then after a while I started thinking about the big women I'd known in my life. A lot of them stoop like it's going to make them look shorter instead of distorted. The big, scary woman cop didn't do that. She seemed happy being so big. Maybe when she wasn't being a cop she could be nice to talk to. I wondered how I would think about her if I met her in Berringers. Probably OK.

Then we arrived at headquarters, and they booked me in and gave me a shirt and put me in a cell alone. I got a cell to myself because I was a murder case. "You're the fourth murderer I've locked up this week," the old guy in charge of the lockup told me as the Dave cop walked me to my cell. The big woman was somewhere else doing the paperwork.

"I'm not a murderer."

"That's what they all say." He laughed with a cackly kind of cough. It made him sound like a chicken-voiced frog.

"I don't care what they all say. I'm no murderer." The old guy didn't care, though, and he put me in the cell and took the handcuffs off and then they left.

The sun was about coming up by then. Some of the guys nearby swore at me for the noise waking them up. "I didn't ask to be here," I said to them, but they just swore some more. Chances were they were murderers too, only real ones.

A couple of kids I knew in high school I heard later killed people. And once, two guys sitting together in Berringers got pointed out to me as gang killers in a hushed voice. Though truth is, I didn't like thinking about murderers. What I did instead was lie down on the bed, and I started thinking about George.

He was killed with the shotgun. I could hardly believe it. Funny to think that only a couple of days ago I was thinking of doing it to him myself the same way. My thinking that all came from seeing what I thought was my truck.

But was it, really?

It had to be, with it being gone when I tried to find it.

Still, no matter what George was doing on shore, my only part was to keep his boat protected while he was away. I guess I did that all right, even if nobody but the kids in the *Sunbird* ever got close enough even to think about damage, unless it was while I was asleep.

But George dead? Wow. I sure bet that wasn't part of his plan for it all. Could it of been one of the people that didn't want his houseboat out there on the lake that did it? If so, then it could even of been me that got killed if I stayed another night. That was not a nice thought when I had it.

But, wouldn't somebody killing George because of the houseboat go on and set fire to it or sink it so it wouldn't be there anymore? I would of, if it was me. So my money would be that George got murdered for something else. Not that I would bet. I need to save all the money I can for Kelly and Little Joe, from now on.

Being murdered made George the first of the bunch of us guys from high school ever to be dead. At least the first that I knew about. It's not like I still saw any of them regularly anymore, not Chuckie or Max, Billy or Ramon. I wondered what happened to them all. Did they do better than me? Or better than George, before he got murdered?

I never noticed when I fell asleep.

They woke me up around seven because of breakfast. And while I was spooning it in, I realized that I didn't dream of women. Maybe I really was on a roll with getting past the habits that were my downfall so much.

Then I wondered if maybe Kelly was going to call me this morning because more than a week was enough punishment. I thought maybe I should use my one phone call to check my messages, but then I decided I wouldn't do that till later in the day. Mornings can be real busy times for Kelly with Little Joe.

Then, a couple of minutes after they took the breakfast tray away the big woman cop from last night came into the row of cells. She was still big, but now she wasn't so scary anymore. Maybe it was because I had a shirt on.

Truth is, I saw how she was well-proportioned with her size, and she walked as if maybe she was athletic. The big women I've liked best were the athletic ones. This woman cop had blonde hair, which I also like. Kelly is blonde.

The woman cop was with a guy and as he unlocked my cell she said, "Your lawyer's here, Prince. Then you and me will have a little talk."

"OK," I said. "Did you ever tell me your name?"

"I'm Sergeant Steponkus."

She cuffed me for the walk out of the cell block. "What kind of name is that?" I asked.

"The kind that's going to fry your murdering ass."

I didn't say anything to that, but some of the other inmates made "oooooo" sounds. I didn't even know they were listening.

Steponkus took me to an interview room. A minute later a tiny little black woman less than five feet tall and skinny with big glasses came in. She set a briefcase on the table and said, "Joseph Prince?"

"Yeah," I said.

Then she said, "Take the cuffs off him, please, Sergeant."

"Are you sure?"

"He's not going to hurt me. You're not going to hurt me, are you, Mr. Prince?"

"Course not."

"Sergeant?"

"It's your neck, Cayenne, but you do know the guy's being held on suspicion of murder."

"Of course I know what he's being held for. Do you think I came in here for a tea party?" The little woman stared at Steponkus with her hand on her hip.

Steponkus went to the door and pointed to a button. "If you have trouble, press this." Then she left.

When we were alone, the little black woman said, "My name is Cayenne Davenport. I'll be your lawyer today."

"Tomorrow too, I hope," I said, "unless I don't need a lawyer by then."

"Wouldn't that be nice." She sat down. "I'll feel more comfortable if I call you Joe and you call me Cayenne. That OK by you?"

"Sure." I figured just about anything she wanted would be OK by me. I liked the way she stood up to Steponkus, even though she was only about a third her size and cute with big brown eyes. I've known some little women over the years. I liked them all. But I tried not to let my mind wander there.

"Sit down, Joe."

"OK." When I sat, she did too, and she took a notebook out of her briefcase.

"There are some ground rules."

"OK."

"The first one is that whatever you say to me must be the truth." She paused. "I guess there's only one ground rule, Joe. Can you cut it?"

"Yup," I said. "Cayenne."

"So, they're looking to charge you with murder . . ."

"They think I killed George, but I didn't do it."

"Then we'll have to see what we can do to get you out of here. We won't be able to go through everything now, though, because Sergeant Steponkus and her colleagues want to do a formal interview with you in a few minutes."

"Good, because I want this whole mess cleaned up as fast as possible. Here I am in jail when I ought to be home in case Kelly and Little Joe come back."

"Kelly and Little Joe?"

"My girlfriend and our baby."

"And when you say 'come back' . . . ?"

"Kelly left me, but I'm going to patch it up as soon as I get out of here." George getting dead was a big reminder that time flies and if you don't hurry, important things can slip you by.

"Well, first why don't you tell me how this situation came about, Joe."

So I began from the beginning with Kelly's witch of a mom not taking me to the funeral in Las Vegas and how that led to Kelly walking out on me with Little Joe and how then I was in Berringers when George came in and hired me to sit on his houseboat and I was out there till I got myself off.

"So you were on this boat for three whole days?"

"Yeah. Till I made a raft to get to shore."

"What did you do on the boat?"

"Guarded it."

"How did you do that?"

"By being there. I watched the boats on the lake sometimes, or the houses on the shore, or I watched the TV. Oh, and sometimes I listened to the radio."

"Steponkus says there were a lot of beer cans on the boat that have your fingerprints on them."

"Yeah, I drank beer, too. George had six-packs out there and it was about the only way I got through the time. Maybe you wouldn't think it's hard being paid to do nothing, but it was.

Truth is, I was missing Kelly."

"You were lonely on the houseboat?"

"Yeah."

"So the dog wasn't the kind of company you were craving?"

I looked at her. "What dog?"

It turned out the way they discovered George's body was when two fishermen went onto the reservoir early in the morning and they heard a dog howling. They went to see where it was, and the dog was on the *Tia Maria*.

When they got there, they saw that it was a big one, and that it was bleeding on its shoulder. It backed away when they got close, but it also growled and snapped, so they got off the *Tia* again and called the local police. Truth is, it took the cops way into the morning to get their act together enough to find a boat and a dog handler to go out. When they finally got to the houseboat they found George's body in the cabin. Then they spent more time deciding whose jurisdiction it was till Steponkus came out from homicide and her people found my fingerprints everywhere, not just the shotgun. Because I already had a record, they thought they had their man.

"So," Cayenne said, "there was no dog with you on the houseboat."

"Right."

"I haven't seen this houseboat, and forgive me for asking, but is there any way the dog could have been on the houseboat without your noticing?"

"No way."

"And the last time you saw George Wayne he was alive?"

"He sure was. He left me on the boat and took the dinghy."

"And Wayne didn't have a dog with him then?"

"No."

"Or at any other time?"

"Nope." I even tried to remember if I ever saw George with a dog in all the years I knew him. I couldn't remember one time.

"So where did the dog on the houseboat come from?" Cayenne asked.

"Beats me," I said.

And then there was a knock on the door and a cop I didn't recognize called us into another room where they wanted to interview me.

Sergeant Steponkus was waiting for us with another guy. She introduced him as Detective Markson, who was a short, dark, frowny kind of guy that looked like he lifted weights. Then Steponkus began the tape recorder and got the interview underway with all the usual stuff about who I was and who they thought I killed.

But it was Cayenne who asked the first real question. "Before we get on to your agenda, Sergeant, what progress have you made on the ownership of the dog?"

Steponkus looked at Markson. "As far as we know it's George Wayne's dog."

"That's not right," I said.

Cayenne put up a finger that I should be quiet again. "My client is very clear on the point that the dog is not his, and that he never saw the dog with the late Mr. Wayne. Did you find anything on the houseboat that would suggest the dog lived there? A water bowl. Dog food. A place to sleep?"

Steponkus and Markson had to say that they didn't.

"Did you find any such items at my client's house?"

They hadn't.

"The reason I'm bringing this point forward," Cayenne said, "is that if the dog was neither Wayne's nor my client's then chances are the dog came to the houseboat with the killer."

"Why would the killer bring a dog and then leave it there?"

Markson asked.

"That's an excellent question for you to discover the answer to."

Markson snorted. "I'll discover it all right. Tell us about the dog, Joe."

"My client knew nothing about the dog until I told him about it," Cayenne said.

"Likely story," Steponkus said.

"Why would my client bring a dog and leave it there?"

"We aren't necessarily saying that's what happened."

"There could be a lot of explanations for the dog," Markson said.

"I'm listening," Cayenne said.

"Maybe the victim only just got it."

"George Wayne acquired a dog, but no dog food?"

"Maybe he fed it off his own plate." Markson shrugged.

Steponkus was thinking. "Where does a dog crap on a houseboat?" she asked Markson. "No newspapers down to train it? No, I don't like the dog as belonging to Wayne."

"Well, maybe the dog is a red herring," Markson said.

"Excuse me?" Cayenne said.

"Maybe the dog fell off somebody else's boat and swam to the houseboat and is nothing to do with this case."

"And just happened to get shot in its shoulder?"

Markson shrugged his own shoulders.

"Is this dog male or female?" Cayenne asked.

Markson looked to Steponkus. "Female," she said.

"And maybe she was beamed down onto the houseboat by aliens," Cayenne said, "but until you produce a little green man, I say that any theory of the crime has to explain the dog. In fact, if you think about it, the dog is probably a key witness in this case."

"A witness?" Steponkus said.

"An identification witness," Cayenne said. "Let's start with basics. Did she have a collar?"

Steponkus looked at Markson who said, "No collar."

"How about a chip?"

"A what?" Markson asked.

Steponkus said, "They can implant identification chips into dogs to keep track of its shots and stuff. Vets can scan them. My sister's dog has one. I should have thought of it before."

Markson shrugged. "We'll take the dog to a vet."

"Where is the dog now?" Cayenne asked.

"The pound."

"They'll have scanners out there."

"We'll check it," Steponkus said.

"Find the owner of that dog and you have a much better suspect than my client."

"Your client's fingerprints are all over the damn murder weapon," Markson said. "That'll usually do it."

"I want to say something about that," I said.

"But before he does," Cayenne said, "I want to know what security arrangements you've made for the dog."

"What do you mean, security arrangements?" Steponkus asked.

"That dog should be under twenty-four-hour armed guard."

"Under what?"

"Think about it. If the dog came to the houseboat with the real killer—which seems the most likely explanation—then the killer knows the dog was left behind. And the killer knows that the dog might be all you need to identify him—or her. Publish a picture of the dog in the papers. Let the TV news people film her. Even if she doesn't have a chip, all it takes is for a neighbor to recognize her."

Steponkus and Markson looked at each other.

Cayenne said, "What if the real killer tries to recover the dog?

Or kill her. Think about what the press will do to you if something happens to the dog. You've got to make very sure she's safe."

Steponkus said, "I'll make sure the dog is safe."

"Can I talk now?" I said. "Because I want to say something about the shotgun."

Everybody turned to me.

I put my hands out. "Isn't there some test they can do to tell if I fired a gun recently? Didn't I see that on TV?"

Cayenne turned to the cops. "My client is volunteering for a gunpowder residue test."

Markson said, "He probably wore gloves."

Cayenne said, "And then took them off to make sure that his fingerprints were all over the shotgun anyway? Your teachers would be so proud."

6

The interview stopped after that. Steponkus told Markson to call a lab person to swab my hands, but as he went out the door he turned back to me and said, "I still think it's your damn dog." And he banged the door as he went out.

"Let's test it," Cayenne said.

"What do you mean?" Steponkus said.

"Do a lineup. Put my client with a bunch of volunteers and see if the dog goes to him."

"You want to do an ID parade for a dog?"

"I saw my client's face when I told him there was a dog on the houseboat. I'm sure he knew nothing about it, but if you harbor the same suspicions as your colleague, then put it to the test." She turned to me. "That OK with you, Joe?"

"Sure," I said.

"Of course it's probably best if you back it up with some kind of expert in dog behavior," Cayenne said. "Someone who'd testify about whether a dog will go to a stranger. Who knows? Maybe some dogs are just sluts."

We sat around not saying a whole lot after that. Then Markson came back with a woman in a white coat. She rubbed a bunch of swabs all over my hands. They kind of tickled.

Once the lab woman left, Markson said, "Even if it's negative, don't think you're walking, Prince. We're still going to test all your clothes."

"OK," I said.

Cayenne said, "I want more time alone with my client now. Why don't you get started with the dog?"

Markson was going to say something, but Steponkus stopped him with a wave. "I guess we can finish this now," she said, so we did.

Cayenne and I went to another room and we had a long talk all about me and George and the houseboat.

"Let's just make this absolutely clear, Joe. George Wayne never told you what he was going to do while he was away from the houseboat?"

"Right."

"Not anything about it?"

"Nothing."

"But from what you saw through the field glasses, you suspect he used your truck without your permission."

"I feel it in here," I said, and I put my hand on my heart. "I just can't prove it."

"Whether Wayne used your truck or not, do you think he might have been doing something illegal?"

"I don't know what else he'd be up to. From a kid, George did a lot of robberies when we were young together. And then the last time I saw him before this time he was scamming the managers of gas stations, which nearly got me into jail."

"How about something that involved violence?"

I thought about that. "He wouldn't mind violence," I said, "but he left the shotgun behind when he left me on the boat."

"He could have had another weapon."

"I was about to say that."

She made some notes. "Would he have worked alone, or did he like working with accomplices?"

"He usually worked with other people if he knew them."

"Is that why he involved you in the gas station scams?"

"He said it was because we were friends in school and he wanted to do me a favor. Some favor."

"Did you know it was illegal when you helped him?"

"No." Then after a minute I said, "Well, maybe. I guess the main thing I think about George is he always tries to find an angle. Like, if he was using my truck the angle would be if people saw it, they'd think it was me and I wouldn't have an alibi."

"Might he have wanted you on the boat so people would think it was him, which would give him an alibi?"

"I didn't think of that." So I thought about the boy and his girlfriend on the *Sunbird*. They never got up close to me. "We are about the same size."

"And age. What about hair color?"

"Mine is darker, but . . ."

"But what?"

"He gave me a hat to wear. A baseball cap, with an anchor on it."

She nodded and made more notes. "I'm asking you all this because I'm going to check police records about the crimes that were committed in the Indianapolis area during the days you were on the houseboat. I'll be looking for something like a rash of Geist area burglaries, or anything else that fits."

That sounded good to me and I said it.

"Next, are you willing for the police to check your truck for fingerprints and any other evidence that Wayne was inside it recently?"

"Sure." I thought about how it had been cleaned. Is it evidence, too, if something's not there?

"The police ought to have done it already, but they ought to have realized the dog was important."

She was smiling now, I guess because she had some ideas to work with. And I saw how pretty she looked, especially when she talked about making the cops take the dog seriously. For just a second there I thought about us, her and me, and wondered how it would be. Did I see any of that look in her eyes?

"Joe?"

"What? Oh. Right."

She started to gather up her things. "That's all for now. I wish I could say you'd be out of here today."

"So do I."

"But meanwhile is there anyone you want me to get in touch with? Kelly, say?"

I hated the idea of Kelly seeing me in a jail, even if it was only for suspicion. "No," I said, "but there is a favor you could do." And I told her how to check my voicemail messages. Maybe Kelly left one or maybe even she already came home.

Then Cayenne knocked for the cop outside to come in and take me back to my cell. "I'll be in touch, Joe."

"Good."

"Keep your pecker up."

But the last thing I wanted was pecker advice from Cayenne. For more than a week now I was doing so well . . .

Back in my cell they gave me a sandwich and some coffee because I missed regular lunch. Then I sat around doing nothing, like I was still on the houseboat in the first place. This time there was no radio and no boats to watch, but there were the other prisoners.

In a jail you think nothing happens, because everybody's locked up. But almost every few minutes someone comes in or they take some guy out. So there are usually things to look at. And they were mean-looking men, these guys. And that was just the guards.

Yuk yuk.

I was feeling better after knowing that my free lawyer was Cayenne. She seemed like a good one.

I must of drifted off for a time lying on my bunk, despite the noise of walking and talking and being unlocked. I know I drifted off because I dreamed of the *Sunbird* again and that little blonde girlfriend. She was sunning herself on the front of the motorboat this time. She turned herself over, and turned herself over again, so she wouldn't burn, or get too hot. Too hot . . .

I woke up sweating.

And I also woke up really hurting for feminine company.

It was the worst wave of it I'd had for days and days. Right then I would of been down at Berringers in a shot if the cell wasn't locked. Right then I didn't care a damn if it was Kelly or not. I wanted someone. I wanted it. I wanted it so bad I even stood up at the bars of my cell and shook them.

Guys nearby shouted, "Shut up!" and other guys laughed. Finally I sat down. It didn't matter what I wanted, I wasn't going to get it. So I tried to get myself back on the track, even though I didn't really feel it.

But before I could think it all through, a guard guy came along and said to me, "Prince, you have a visitor."

That scared me for a minute, because the last person I wanted to see right then was Cayenne. Because I'd be really glad to see her, if you know what I mean.

"Move it, Prince. Whatsa matter?" the guy said.

But she was my lawyer who was getting me out of here, so I got up and had to do it. "I'm coming," I said. Only I regretted saying that, too.

The guard put handcuffs on me and led me out of the holding cells and turned me over to a cop I didn't know. This time we didn't take the same route to an interview room as before, and I was glad of the extra walk to calm me down and get me ready to think of new ideas about the dog and George and whatnot. Maybe they had a lineup ready.

When finally we got to a room, the cop sat me at a table and then he stood in a corner. It wasn't but a minute before I heard people outside, and the door opened. Standing there was Kelly.

Kelly! I could hardly believe it. I jumped up.

A cop said to her, "You got fifteen minutes."

"OK," Kelly said.

She was so beautiful. Ten minutes would of been long enough for twice. I was soo sorry I'd even given a minute to thinking about Cayenne, who wasn't a patch on Kelly to me.

"Oh, honey," I said and I reached out to her in my handcuffs and began to come around the table, only the cop in the corner stepped in my way and said, "No physical contact, except over the table."

The table would of been just fine with me, but that wasn't what he meant. And I also saw that Kelly herself had moved back from me when I moved her way. "Kell?" I said. "Are we OK again?"

She twitched a shoulder, like she does when she's not sure of something. "I don't know if I ought to be here, Joe."

"You should. You should. I am so happy to see you, baby. I can't begin to tell you how happy."

She didn't say anything, but I could see that she was glad to see me underneath, too, because she glanced at the cop in the corner like he was restraining us.

"Where's Little Joe?" I said as I sat down again.

"He's with Momma. I didn't want to bring him . . . You know, here." She sat down too.

"Uh huh." I nodded. "But how did you know I was here? Did Cayenne tell you after all?"

"Cayenne? Who is Cayenne, Joseph?"

"The lawyer they assigned to me. I mean my case. She's for free."

"Oh." She folded her arms on her chest.

"I told her not to tell you where I was."

She shook her head like I was an idiot. "You're in the newspapers, Joe. And on the TV."

"I'm on the TV?"

"Momma saw it. She said you were arrested, for killing George."

"I'm not arrested. I'm just on suspicion."

"But George? How could that be, Joe?"

"He came into Berringers and—"

"You were in Berringers?"

"Just for a drink. Honest. I've haven't been with anybody for—how many days is it since you left? Nobody. Not one. Not once. I didn't go out with anybody but George from Berringers—you can ask Eileen that works there. And from that time to this I've been working really hard to grow up and have a more mature attitude like you said. And it's all because I love you so much, Kelly. Truth is, I think about you just about all the time. Everything I do and everything I don't do is all for you."

I could tell that someplace inside she was being pleased. And I was real happy to have a chance to tell her about the progress I made. "Oh, baby," I said.

"You didn't have to kill George for me, Joe. Not kill him."

There was something about the way she said it that made me stop and look at her face.

"Just cutting his nuts off would have done." She did a little giggle, and it showed she was nervous about something.

"What are you saying, Kell?"

"Nothing."

"Something about you, and George?"

73

"I ran into him, that's all."

"You ran into him?"

"Don't shout, Joe." She looked over at the cop in the corner. I'd forgotten about him, but I didn't really care. "What do you mean you ran into him? When did you run into him?"

"It was on the day after I took Little Joe to Momma's."

"You ran into him the same day after you left me?"

"Jo-oe," she said, nodding to the cop again.

"Tell me, Kell."

"It was an accident. A coincidence. I was coming out of the Kroger and there he was. Him and Chuckie."

"You ran into George and Chuckie? Chuckie from the old days?"

"What other Chuckie do we know that isn't in the movies?"

"Where did you run into them?"

"At the Kroger."

"The Kroger in the old neighborhood?"

"Yeah. Well, outside. It was in the parking lot. C'mon, Joe, I have to shop. Momma doesn't keep the stuff in her house I need to look after Little Joe right."

"And where was Little Joe at this time?"

"With Momma. She's taking days off work because we're there."

I didn't say anything to that for a minute. I wouldn't trust Kelly's mom to look after Little Joe even if he was asleep. Then I said, "So what about George and Chuckie? What did they want?"

"Nothing. Well . . ."

I sighed about as loud as a hurricane. "George and Chuckie? I mean, Chuckie." We knew that Chuckie would go after every female woman that ever crossed his path.

"Nothing happened, Joe. And it wasn't Chuckie. It was George that was rude. Chuckie was the perfect gentleman. He

even shouted at George and made him go away after I had to
hit him."

I jumped up, about ready to murder that fucking George
Wayne, only then I remembered that somebody already did.

"Joe!" Kelly stood up too.

And the cop in the corner moved our way.

"Nothing happened?" I said. "Tell me about the nothing that
didn't happen."

"Calm down first."

"I'm calm."

"No, you're not." She looked deep into my face.

And when I looked back, I saw in her eyes the look that I
wanted to see. The look that said that we were back together
again and she'd be back after all this was over. So I calmed
down, and sat down, and I took deep breaths and I said, "Sorry,
Kell. Sorry, baby." Her pretty blonde hair was tied up on her
head, but in my brain I could see it down and hanging loose. "I
love you so much."

"I know you do."

"I really am sorry. About . . . Well about everything. What
happened. And about being in this place and not being able to
come home right now to you and Little Joe."

She sat still for a minute before she said, "You really didn't
know about George grabbing my tit?"

George Wayne was lucky he was already murdered, no fool-
ing. "Just tell me, Kell."

"OK. So I come out of the Kroger into the parking lot and
there's George and Chuckie, only I don't see them at first. What
I see is this car, and I happen to look at it because it was a
Volkswagen—one of those Jettas I like. You know, with that
color that seems like it's blue sometimes but then other times
it's purple? It's like you have two cars even though you only
have the one."

"Kell . . ."

"OK, OK. So I'm looking at the car, but then I see there are two guys in it and I realize they're George and Chuckie. So I stop because I can't believe it. And when I stop, they see me, too. And then they both get out and we all say, like, George? Chuckie? Kelly? You know, like you do."

"What about George, Kell? Tell me about George."

"Yeah, all right, keep your hair on. Well, you already know what I think about George."

I knew that, all right.

"Anyhow, they say, Chuckie I think it was. He says, 'What are you doing in the old neighborhood?' And all I say is that I'm staying with Momma in her new apartment. But then George says, 'You mean you've left Joe?' and he has this smirk on his face. But I have to say that I don't know for sure if I've left you. You know, left you. Because I'm still fed up with how you act, Joe, how I can't be away from you for half an hour."

"It was days you were away for, Kell. Days."

"At my grandfather's funeral, for Christ's sake. You could have shown some respect."

"You never even knew him."

"I had to go. Momma needed me there."

"She'll take any damn excuse to get you loose from me."

"You're right about that one."

I didn't remember her agreeing with me before. "I am?"

"Do you know what Momma says now? She says if I've finally come to my senses and left you for good, especially now that you're in prison, she says that she'll put the money up for me to start my personal trainer business."

"She said that?"

"And you know how bad that's what I want to do, don't you?"

I did, but I didn't want to say it. Instead I said, "What I knew was she had plenty of money to take me along to the funeral too, if she'd of wanted to."

"It's her inheritance money she's talking about, Joe. She's willing to invest it in me. She believes in me."

"I believe in you, Kelly. And you know if I had the money . . ."

"I know. I know." She shook her head in a sad way. "And I didn't say I was going to take Momma's offer. I'm just telling you the how of how things are. Even if it's not the right time to talk about it, but you did go and start about the damn funeral again."

She was right. I should of shut up about that, because it was over now. And, truth is, Kelly came to see me in jail without me even asking. That meant a lot, even if I never wanted her to see me here. "You're right, Kell. I'm sorry."

"Are you?"

"I really am. Sorry about saying all that again. And . . . about everything."

"OK." She ran her hand through her pretty hair, which she knows I like her to do. "So, do you want me to finish telling you this?"

"Yeah."

"So George and Chuckie and me are in this parking lot. And by now they're together in front of the Jetta, and for a minute they whisper together and I'm about to say goodbye. But then George steps away from the car in my direction. And he says, 'You always were a sweet piece of ass, Kelly,' and I say, 'Excuse me,' and he says how I should be nice to him because he's got money now and he's going to have plenty more."

"Bastard," I said.

"And then before I knew it he put one arm around me and grabbed my tit with the other hand and he stuck his big old stinky mouth in my face and tried to stick his tongue in. So I smacked him one."

"You hit him?"

77

"And you know how strong I am, Joe."

I knew that, all right.

"And I caught him a good one, and it knocked him on his own damn piece of ass."

"I sure would of liked to see that." Even though I hated the idea of George's hand and his stinky tongue.

"So then Chuckie stood over George like he was angry and he told George not to think with his dick all the time. And when George got up again Chuckie gave him a shove and told him to get out of here, so George got back in his car, which was the nice Jetta. And he drove away."

"Good riddance," I said.

"So you can see, Joe, when I heard what happened to George and how they had you in jail, I thought you must have heard about what he did with me and that's why you did it. Maybe Chuckie told you, or something."

"I haven't seen Chuckie for years."

"But I still had to come in, when I thought that, didn't I? I had to come in to say you didn't have to kill him for that, even though I sure don't mind him being dead, because you know what I think about George Wayne. Or thought about him, I mean, rest his soul."

"I didn't know what happened at the Kroger, baby, but if I did know then maybe the end sure would of been the same."

She looked at me then. I could see she remembered the me she still loved.

"I miss you so bad, honey," I said.

"And I miss you."

"And you will come back home when I get out of here, won't you? You and Little Joe?"

"Course we will."

"Because I never did it, Kell. I didn't even know about it till the cops came to the house to bring me in for suspicion."

"I know you didn't, Joe. I thought maybe you did, but I knew you didn't really."

"Good."

"So will you be out of here soon, do you think?"

"I sure hope so. See, there's this dog that was on the houseboat where George got killed and . . . Well, truth is, it's a long story, and it's not all that clear yet. But the dog may be a witness for me."

"What dog, Joe? Not a German shepherd?"

"I don't know what kind of a dog. I never saw it. Why?"

"Cause Chuckie had a dog."

"He did?"

"A big German shepherd dog. It was in the backseat of his car."

"I thought the car was George's."

"That car was. But Chuckie had his own, a Ford. A green one. And there was a dog in the back."

"When did you see Chuckie's car?"

"He followed me home."

"He what?"

"He followed me back to Momma's. At least to the parking lot behind her block."

"Why did he do that?"

"He said it was because he wanted to be sure that George didn't try to hook up with me again, because George doesn't like it when he doesn't get what he wants."

"For that, Chuckie went home with you?"

"Just into the parking lot. He never even got out of his car again. He did offer to carry my bags in, though."

"I bet he did."

"But I said no, Joe. And when I was safe at the door he drove away. It didn't feel like he was hitting on me."

"If you say so." But it still all seemed strange to me. Because the Chuckie I knew from the old days was never the guy in the gang who would ever do anything for anybody unless it was for himself, too. And usually it was easy to see what he was after, especially with a girl. And Chuckie was one of the guys I knew longest, along with Max, even from grade school.

But I never got the chance to ask Kelly more about it because then the cop from outside the room came in again and said, "You've had your fifteen minutes, Miss. Say goodbye and let's go."

Kelly and I stood right up then and didn't say anything more but just stretched across the table and kissed each other until the cop from the outside and the cop in the corner both had to drag us apart.

It was about the best kiss I ever had in my life. And it was also about the worst, because we couldn't follow it up. I wanted her soo bad. Soooo bad.

7

The whole long walk back to my cell I suffered from missing Kelly so much. It wasn't till they took the cuffs off and locked the door behind me and I sat on the bunk that I began to think about the other things that Kelly said and what they might mean.

Like George coming into Berringers asking me whatever happened to Kelly like he'd never seen her for years when the truth is he'd just tried to stick his stinky tongue in her mouth that same afternoon. I started sweating, thinking about that, I was so glad the bastard was already dead.

Still, he did have that nasty red mark on the side of his head, like somebody hit him. Because somebody did.

And then I thought of how George said in Berringers he swore he hoped to run into me there that night. At the time I took it as a complete coincidence. But the truth is after he ran into Kelly in the Kroger parking lot in the old neighborhood, he worked out that I might go for a drink that night in Berringers because he knew my habits.

So it was no accident he picked me for the guy to sit on his houseboat, even though that kind of thing is better when it's someone you know. And I own a truck.

The bastard. At least he was a bastard with a mark on his face where he got hit. Kelly is strong, and not just for her little size. She works at it and that's one of the reasons I keep in shape with workouts too, plus my own job of lifting.

But truth is, I just didn't believe George would ever of thought he could have a chance with Kelly. She hated him and she wasn't shy to say it. He was never going to have a chance without it being rape, so it was a mystery why he ever tried it with her in the first place in the parking lot with Chuckie there.

And Chuckie was another mystery. Why would a guy like Chuckie follow Kelly home for no good reason?

And then I got it.

Chuckie followed Kelly home to know where she was living. He'd of known where Freda, Kelly's mom used to live in the old days but not since she moved to the new apartment. That must of been it.

And he'd of wanted to know where she lived because Kelly saw him with George, which would be the two of them plotting a crime together. So it would of been Chuckie who was the other guy loading stuff from houses into my truck that I saw through the field glasses. Or something else that was the two of them, if it turned out the truck I saw wasn't mine.

I sure wished now that I'd looked around at the cars when I went to where my truck wasn't. If I'd of noticed a blue-purple Jetta or a green Ford nearby, that would of iced the proof that they took my truck and only brought it back when I was asleep.

It made sense. George sent me out to the houseboat to get my truck but also to keep me from talking to Kelly and putting two and two together in case I worked it out he was doing a crime with Chuckie. And it had to be a crime because Chuckie was a big criminal from our high school gang, probably the biggest.

Morg White was the first of us all to go to jail, but Chuckie was the first one that used a gun to hold up a gas station and he laughed about it after. Him and George wouldn't of been planning anybody's birthday party, that's for sure.

So Chuckie followed Kelly home to know where she lived.

Because she was a witness to them.

And she was a witness to Chuckie having a dog.

I put my hands on my face. Oh shi-it.

I didn't know what kind of a dog the one left on the houseboat was, but I'd sure bet good money now it was a big German shepherd. I still didn't know why Chuckie left the dog on the boat with George, but Chuckie knew why he left it. And he knew Kelly could connect a dog and George and him all together. Maybe she was the only one.

I ran to the bars of my cell and rattled them as hard as I could. "Let me out of here," I shouted. "I got to talk to somebody, quick. Come on! Come on!"

About the only fast response I got was from other guys in cells laughing or telling me to shut up or else getting up to run tin cups along their bars to make noise too.

"Guard! Guard!" I shouted and kept shouting.

Kelly was a witness to put them all together, and if Chuckie already murdered George, he wasn't about to stop at murdering Kelly.

"Guard! Guard! Guard!"

Finally an old fat guy came waddling along the corridor. "What the fuck is your problem, Prince?"

"Kelly's in danger. I got to protect her. I got to get out of here."

He looked at me like I was crazy, and meanwhile other guys in their cells heard Kelly's name and started repeating it up and down the corridor like it was a joke.

But I worked it out that the fat old guy didn't know what I was talking about. Of course. He was just a fat old guy. I said, "I need to talk to someone, right away. It's important. It's life or death."

"Talk to Dirty Dom."

"Who?"

"The perv in the cell next to yours. He killed four people. He knows life and death."

"Bullshit," the guy in the cell next to mine said.

"I don't mean talk to him," I said. "I need to talk to my lawyer."

"What's the rush? You ain't going nowhere."

"Or Steponkus. I'll talk to her. Sergeant Steponkus, quick."

"What the fuck for? You gonna confess?"

"Yeah, yeah. I'll confess. That's it. I want to confess right now, but if it isn't right now I won't do it. So get Steponkus in here, because she'll kick your ass if you don't let me confess to her when it's her one and only chance."

The fat old guy stood looking at me.

"Why are you just standing there?" I said. "Go get her."

"You're sure you're going to confess?"

"Yeah, I'm going to confess."

"Confess to murdering the guy you murdered?"

"Yeah, him."

"Because if you don't, I'm a gonna make your life a living hell when they bring you back here."

"I want to confess. Let me confess."

Someone down the hall shouted out, "Let him confess, for Christ's sake, Willie. It's time for *All Things Considered*. How can I listen with all this noise going on?"

So the old fat guy said, "Wait here. I'll see if I can find Steponkus." And he waddled away.

Where the hell else was I going to wait?

"Faster!" I shouted after him, because I couldn't help myself. But he didn't look back. He just gave me the finger.

I spent the whole time he was away hopping up and down. For all I knew Chuckie could be murdering Kelly right now while all this nothing was going on. I just couldn't keep still. And what about Little Joe? Who would look after him if Kelly was dead. Not her witch of a mom, that's for sure. Over my dead body.

Or would Chuckie kill Little Joe, too? Was he the crazy kind of guy to do that now? I wouldn't put it past him.

I couldn't bear it. I rattled the bars on my cell door. I rattled the bars on the cell window, even though there was glass outside of them.

Truth is, Chuckie always was an evil bastard. Underneath his smiles, and his being part of the gang, he had a cruelty streak. I always knew it. I just never really cared when we were a gang and the cruelty didn't aim at me. But even as a gang there were times that some of us had to pull him off somebody because he would take it too far if we didn't.

Yeah, as soon as Chuckie was in the picture it was obvious who killed George, even if I didn't know why. Except I bet it was money. Chuckie always liked to have more money than anybody else to spend and impress people and women with, because he wasn't a big guy, and he wasn't good looking. He even worked out at a gym and lifted weights before any of the rest of us to be more impressive.

So what happened was that when it came time for Chuckie and George to divide up what they stole, Chuckie liked the idea of having it all instead of fair-shares? Could that be how it happened? Would Chuckie do something like that?

Well, I couldn't say that he wouldn't.

And then I thought of a reason why he might of thought it was safe to go and kill George and get away with it. Maybe it was because he knew I was on the houseboat and my fingerprints would be all over the place. Maybe Chuckie had the idea of pinning it on me all along.

And truth is, working that out calmed me down some. Because as long as Chuckie thought I was getting blamed for the murder, he didn't have to rush to kill Kelly as a witness, especially if we were broken up and she didn't care what happened to me anymore anyway. Maybe me being in jail now and in the papers and on the TV was already why he hadn't done anything to Kelly yet. Because if he'd wanted to he already had nearly a couple of days since he killed George. And he did know where she was living with her mom.

Oh God.

Unless that only meant he was planning to take his time.

I stood at the bars on my cell and shook them and shook them and shook them.

At last the door at the end of the corridor opened and I could see the fat old guy, Willie, come in. He was followed by the other detective, Markson.

"Where's Sergeant Steponkus?" I said when they got close enough.

"She's out," Markson said. "Seeing a man about a fucking dog, as a matter of fact."

"The dog doesn't matter anymore."

"Oh no?" Markson said. "Well, you better tell that to your lawyer, because as far as she's concerned anything short of the witness protection program won't be good enough."

"It doesn't matter," I said. "I know whose dog it is now. And I know who murdered George."

Markson shook his head, like to clear it. "What's going on, Prince? I thought you wanted to confess." He turned to the fat old man. "Willie?"

"It's what he told me, Pete. Even Dirty Dom'll tell you. He heard." Willie pointed into the cell next to mine.

I couldn't see the guy in there but I heard him say, "I ain't testifying to nothing without I get immunity from the rest of it."

"From four murders? Yeah, right," Markson said.

"I didn't do them murders. Not all of them."

"Can it, Dominic." Markson turned back to me. "You. Prince. Are you ready to confess now, or not?"

"I have things I need to tell you," I said.

"Well, why don't you tell 'em to Dominic, because I sure as hell don't have the time to shoot the breeze."

"Real important things." I was about at my edge.

"I got things to do." He turned around and headed for the door. "It's amazing, Willie," he said to the fat old guy. "Last week it was murders, this week we're up to our asses in armed robberies."

"I'm confessing, I'm confessing." He kept walking. "I did it. It was me!"

Markson stopped. As he made his way back to my cell he said, "What about your lawyer?"

"What about her?"

"You want her there while you do it?"

Getting to talk to Cayenne would be good. "Yeah."

Markson sighed. "I'll be back for him in a while, Willie. Don't let him hang himself." He turned away again.

"Hey! Hey!" I called. "Where are you going?"

"To try to find your fucking lawyer."

"No. Wait. I don't want my lawyer."

He turned back to me. "Yes or no?"

"Yes. Or no. Whatever you mean. But I don't want my lawyer. I don't need my lawyer to confess. I just want to do it now."

"You heard him, Willie."

"I heard he don't want his lawyer, Pete."

"You, too, huh, Dom?" Markson called while Willie got out the handcuffs and opened up my cell.

"I din't heard nothing without my immunity," Dom said.

"You'll be immune, all right," Markson said, "once they get you to Terre Haute. Immune from everything."

"Ain't nobody injecting me," Dom said.

"I'll do it myself with a big smile on my face," Markson said. "We ready to go, Willie?"

"Yeah."

Once we got to the end of the lockup Markson took me into an interview room. "Wait here," he said. "And don't think you can fucking break the place up or anything. I'll be back in like a minute."

"I don't want to wait a minute."

"Well, ain't that a shame. Because you'll wait two minutes or even three if I say so. Do you think we organize things for the convenience of fucking murderers? Now sit down and shut up."

"I didn't murder anyone," I said.

Markson turned back from where he was leaving at the door. "What?" I saw in his face he was angry.

"I said I'd confess and I will. And I want you to arrest me for the murder, not just suspect me anymore, so it can go into the papers and the TV that you arrested me. Because that's what will keep Kelly safe from Chuckie."

He squinted, thinking until he said, "Who the fuck is Chuckie?"

"Chuckie's the real murderer. And Kelly's the one who knows it's his dog, and who also saw George and Chuckie together."

"Wait. Wait." He held his hand up to stop me.

But now I was started telling him about what I worked out I kept on telling him until he heard it all.

Somewhere in it Markson decided to listen to me. What he was interested in most was that somebody was with George before he was killed who had a dog.

When finally I got it all out I finished by saying, "You and Sergeant Steponkus never told me what kind of dog it was on the houseboat, right?"

I could see him try to remember.

But I didn't wait for him. "Kelly says the dog she saw was like a German shepherd. A big one. So tell me, the dog that's the witness, is it like a German shepherd?"

"Yeah," Markson said. "As a matter of fact, it is."

"So that proves it." I made a fist like I won something.

"You could have found out about the dog from someone else."

"I didn't. I got it from Kelly."

"Even so, what I don't understand," he said, "is why the fuck you didn't tell us about this Kelly this morning?"

"I didn't know she saw George or any of the rest of it when I talked to you and Steponkus. Kelly only came in to see me this afternoon."

He sighed, but he took out a pen. "So where does this Kelly live?"

"Where she lives is with me, of course," I said, "but where she's staying at the minute is with her mom." And I gave him the address of the apartment block and the number, 3K.

And while I was saying it, I realized that Chuckie probably didn't know which apartment because he wouldn't know Kelly's mom's new last name, which was her maiden one after Kelly's dad left for good and she sold the house. That would slow him down. Though if he wanted to, he could always ask around for which apartment had a beautiful blonde with a baby staying in it with an old witch.

Or he could hang around in the parking lot till Kelly came out. He didn't know the apartment, but he did know Kelly's car.

"Prince!" Markson was shouting at me.

"What?"

"I said, I'm going to go talk to this Kelly of yours now."

"Hurry. She's in danger."

"So you say."

"Chuckie could already be after her. He could even of been waiting outside her mom's for when she got back from visiting me here. So can't we call her now, to make sure she's still all right? I haven't called anybody since I got here. And I am allowed one phone call. Right?"

We went into the room the homicide detectives work from. I sat in a chair by Markson's desk while he dialed the number for Kelly's mom.

I would of had him do the talking anyway, though he didn't ask, because the old witch would probably hang up the minute she heard my voice before we knew if Kelly was safe or not.

But when Markson talked, it was to frown and say, "Who is this?" Then after a minute he said, "This is Detective Peter Markson, calling from IPD. You're saying there's been a fire?"

I jumped up and would of grabbed the phone if Markson hadn't pushed me away and told me to shut up. To the phone he said, "You're talking arson, or a wastebasket fire, or what?"

Then he sat still listening to who was talking and the only thing that kept me where I was was the furious, angry look on his face. It about drove me crazy when he said things like, "Just the one?" and "Anybody else in the apartment?" At last he said thanks to the phone and goodbye.

I had to jump up again. I couldn't help myself. But he wouldn't say anything to me till I sat down again, so I did.

"The fire department is there. A smoke detector went off and after a while a neighbor came over to see what was happening. The neighbor smelled smoke and called 911."

"What about Kelly?"

"The guy I talked to says a woman was found on the floor in the apartment, but she isn't a young woman. She's blonde, but middle-aged and chubby."

"That's Freda, Kelly's mom. What about Kelly and Little Joe?"

"No one else was there. The woman they found has a head injury. Maybe she was hit, or could be she slipped or something. Anyway, a fire started in the kitchen. Could be arson, or not. They don't know yet. But the injured woman's on her way to the hospital. He doesn't know how badly hurt she is."

"But there was no baby in the apartment? No other woman?"

"No one else, the guy said."

I thought about that for a minute.

Markson said, "Do you know where your Kelly might be?"

"She might of gone home with Little Joe. We made up again when she came in to see me here."

"Good. We can check that out."

"Or but," I said, "it could be that Chuckie already found her and Little Joe at the apartment and took them away with him." That's what I was really afraid of, because the more I remembered about Chuckie, the worse it was.

8

Markson let me call to my own phone at home. I hoped and hoped that Kelly would answer it, but all I got was the voice-mail again. That didn't prove anything. She might of not got there yet, like maybe she went shopping first to get things for Little Joe. There were a lot of things she could of done that weren't being kidnapped by Chuckie.

I left a message to say, "Kelly, you and Little Joe got to get out of the house right away cause it's not safe from Chuckie. I can explain it all later, but now you should come downtown to the police station. Or if you go someplace else, there's a cop you should call named Markson. His number is . . ." And Markson dictated his number to me to leave on the message.

After I hung up, Markson said, "Tell me, does this Chuckie know where you live?"

I thought about it. I only moved to the house after the gang all split up. I sure didn't know where any of them lived. "I don't think so."

"So chances are Kelly and Little Joe would be safe there at home."

"Not if Chuckie beat it out of Kelly's mom where we live," and I could see that Markson didn't think of that. Then I said, "Are there cops over at Kelly's mom's for the fire?"

"There should be, unless they've left already."

"Because if there is a cop there, you could say to look in the parking lot behind the building for Kelly's car."

I saw him work out for himself that if Kelly's car was gone then probably she drove away someplace herself, but if her car was still there then maybe she was in Chuckie's car. Markson picked up his phone again.

And it was then I saw Sergeant Steponkus. She was walking into the homicide room from the corridor. She saw me, too, and came over. Her face was puzzled. "What's up?" she asked when she got to me, and by then Markson was talking on his phone.

I said, "He's finding if Kelly's car is behind her mom's building from one of the cops that went there because of the fire, if he's still there."

"Say what?"

"I guess you don't know yet about all the stuff that's happened."

But before I could tell her, Markson got off the phone. "One of our guys is going out back to look. He'll call me."

"I've got the dog set up at Doggie Hilton," Steponkus said. "So what the hell's going on here?"

"Quite a lot." Markson looked over to a cop sitting at the next desk. "Homer, this guy here is Joe Prince. He's a murder suspect. I need to talk to Steph a few minutes without taking Prince back to the lockup. If I leave him here, will you keep an eye on him, and shoot him in the heart if he gets out of his fucking chair?"

Homer looked up. "His heart instead of his brain?"

"Brain if you're looking for a challenge."

Homer took his gun out from under his arm and put it on his desk.

"Stay in your chair," Markson told me. "In the chair. Understand?"

I nodded. "But if Chuckie's got Kelly—"

"I want to bring Sergeant Steponkus up to speed while we're

waiting for news from the parking lot, but the sooner I start the sooner we'll decide what to do."

"If your phone rings, do you want me to answer it?" I glanced at Homer. "I can do it without getting off the chair if I stretch."

"Leave my fucking phone alone." Markson held up a cell phone to show me, but then he just turned away to take Steponkus someplace privater.

"Make sure it's turned on!" I called after him.

I saw Homer look up at me.

"It's an important call," I said. "It could be life or death."

But then I looked away. I didn't want to think about it being life or death for Kelly. If something happened to Kelly from all this I'd about burst. The idea of me without Kelly . . . The idea of Little Joe without a mom . . .

But then I worked out that even if Kelly's car was still parked in the lot it didn't have to mean she was kidnapped by Chuckie. She could of taken Little Joe for a walk in his stroller. Or she could of gone to visit someone else in her mom's building, even if I didn't know who it was. Or she could even of taken her mom's car off somewhere. Or . . .

It seemed forever before Markson and Steponkus got back, but when they did Markson said, "Kelly's car isn't there."

"He's sure?"

"She's sure," he said, but he smiled. "I asked the same thing."

"We need to find your Kelly as fast as we can," Steponkus said, and I was real glad to hear that. "She doesn't have a cell phone, I take it."

"No."

"So either she's on her way to your house, or she went out and will come back to her mother's. That's right, isn't it, Joe? There's no other place she'd go?"

"Not unless Chuckie took her in her own car."

Steponkus looked at Markson, then back to me. "Why would he do that?"

"I didn't say he would, unless his own broke down or he didn't want anybody looking for it. Did your cop at the fire say if there was a green Ford around there?"

"I didn't ask," Markson said.

"One of us should go to the mother's building," Steponkus said to Markson, "and the other should go to Joe's house."

"Agreed."

I said, "You should also call up to the place that keeps car records." They turned to look at me. "To get Chuckie's license plate number from it being a green Ford and him being Chuckie Gardner. And it would give you an address too, wouldn't it? Even if it maybe isn't the right one for him at the minute."

"We do want to talk to Chuckie," Markson said.

"Yeah," Steponkus said.

"I'll see what I can get on his car."

"OK. You go to the fire scene. I'll go to the house. But keep in touch."

"Sure," Markson said. "But what about him?" He meant me.

Steponkus scratched her head a minute while I said, "What about me?"

Markson said, "He is the only one who knows Kelly and Chuckie by sight."

"I guess," Steponkus said. "What do you say, Joe? If I take you with me instead of sending you back to the lockup, will you do exactly what I tell you, no more, no less?"

"You bet," I said. "Cross my heart," and I did. The idea of being somewhere out of jail was wonderful to me.

"Make sure you do," Homer said from his desk. "Cause if you don't she's gonna plug you in your heart and your brain. She's a hell of a shot and she's killed two men already."

"One of them was only little," Steponkus said. "Does he still count?"

I went with Steponkus to her car in the police basement and she put me in the backseat. I still had handcuffs on, and she told me the doors wouldn't open from the inside. I couldn't care less. She was taking me where I wanted to go.

But before we set out from the garage she took out a cell phone. She looked at a notebook and dialed a number but only pushed the last button when we were out on Alabama Street.

A minute later she said, "This is Steponkus. Yeah, hi. Look, I know you said you wanted to see your client again today, but I've got him in the backseat of my cruiser right now, and we're on our way over to his house." After a minute she said, "No, he hasn't been released. Yeah, yeah, well if you'll give me a chance." Then after another minute, "There have been some developments, having to do with his lady friend, Kelly. We need to talk with her because it seems she saw the deceased together with a guy called Chuckie Gardner, and this Chuckie Gardner had a dog with him who's maybe the same as our dog." After a minute, "Gardner's an old friend of your client's." Then, "Yeah, totally voluntary." She leaned back toward me. "You're out here with me because you want to be, right, Joe?"

"Yes," I said. Then, in case Cayenne didn't hear me, I shouted it the second time.

Steponkus listened some more and then she passed the phone back to me. "Your lawyer wants a word."

I took the phone and said, "Hello?"

"Even if their attitude to you seems to be changing, be very careful about what you say to them, Joe."

"OK."

"I will try to get over to your house, but I may not be able to make it for a while. Is the address I have on file the right one?"

And she read me my own address.

"It sure is," I said. I was glad I was going to see Cayenne. It was really good how much she was working for my case, because the last time the lawyer they gave me for free was always lazy and slow. "But we might have to go someplace else if Kelly shows up at her mom's instead. Did you hear about the fire?"

"What fire?"

So I told her about the fire and that led on to the rest of what had happened, about Chuckie and George and Kelly and Chuckie's dog.

"Well, well, well," she said when I was about done with it all. "Pass the phone back to the good sergeant now, Joe."

So I did and I looked out the window while they were talking. Talking about the fire got me nervous again for what might of happened to Kelly. It was not a good feeling.

By the time Steponkus was done talking with Cayenne we were already about on my street. We didn't go straight in to the house, though. Steponkus drove slowly around the block first, in case we could see Kelly's car or Chuckie's, but they weren't there. So she parked halfway down the block.

Steponkus's car was a plainclothes one. You could tell it was police from the aerial and by looking inside. But someone not looking for a cop car might not notice it in the crowd.

We were also careful walking down the street, and on the porch, and opening the door. I thought it might be in case of scaring Kelly or waking up Little Joe if he was asleep, but then I worked out she was probably thinking more about if Chuckie was already in the house.

But inside no one was there. It was good that it wasn't Chuckie, but I also felt disappointed and like a big cloud settled on my head because Kelly and Little Joe weren't already there and safe. There wasn't even a note left for me to say she'd been home and was coming back later. The only note was what I wrote for her in the first place all those days ago. Even having the police in there didn't move it.

After we looked around to see for sure there was no sign of Kelly and Little Joe I didn't know what would happen next, so I asked Steponkus.

But she just waved at me to sit down and she took out her phone again and soon she said, "Whazzup, Pete?"

She listened for a while and even though I really really wanted to, I didn't ask what Markson was saying as it all went along.

Then she said, "What about the victim? Any news? Like maybe she woke up and told someone what happened?" And, "Well, put out a city-wide on Gardner's car. And while we're about it . . . Hang on a sec." She turned to me. "Joe, do you know Kelly's plate number?"

I did and I told it to her.

"And is Kelly's last name Kovic, like her mother's, or the same as yours, or what?"

"It's Bishop," I said. "She was married and divorced right out of high school. It was a big mistake."

She told it to Markson and told him to have Kelly's car stopped too, which seemed a good idea to me, but I said, "Tell them to be real careful about it if there's a guy in the car."

"What?"

I said it again, "Because if there's a guy it's probably Chuckie." I didn't like to think of that, but it was better to think about it than have something bad happen because I didn't.

Steponkus nodded and said it to Markson, and some other things.

I was thinking how if Chuckie was in a car with Kelly at all, it would be better for it to be Kelly's car because no way would Chuckie have the right kind of safety seat for a baby like we had. Even if he had a special seat for his dog, it wouldn't be the same.

Steponkus said to Markson, "We'll wait it out here unless something's happening at the hospital." When she was done on the phone, to me she said, "There's no sign of Kelly's car or Charles Gardner's car behind the apartment building. Markson's going to keep some of our guys at the scene. They'll go around to the neighbors to see if anybody was asking questions to find Mrs. Kovic's apartment before the fire. At the same time they'll keep an eye out for Kelly and the cars. Meanwhile he'll come over here, unless . . ."

She dialed her phone again. This time it was to the hospital where they took Kelly's mom and the cop who was there with her. She asked him what the news at the hospital was.

While they were talking I thought about how upset Kelly would be when she heard about her mom. Because of that I hoped Freda would get better from it all, even though she was still an old witch who hated me. After what happened with George and my being in the newspapers and on the TV, she sure wasn't going to like me any better.

Finally Steponkus finished on the phone. "The woman we're assuming is Kelly's mother is still unconscious. She's breathing on her own, but they're going to do a scan to see if they can assess the damage to her brain. At the moment it's going ahead on the police budget, but we will eventually need Kelly to help us get information about her mother's insurance. Unless you know something about that?"

"No."

"Or is there someone else? Is there a friend who would know? Or does Kelly have sisters or brothers we could contact?"

"Kelly's brother is in Arizona somewhere, but I don't even know if Kelly knows where, unless they got back in touch at the funeral."

Steponkus said, "There doesn't seem to be much chance Mrs. Kovic will be able to talk to us anytime soon. So we might as well wait here in case Kelly comes home, or returns to the apartment." And she made another call, to the dispatcher to say for all calls to be put through to her cell.

When Steponkus was done, I said, "How about you call Markson now and tell him to bring some KFC when he comes here?" I was getting hungry and I knew there wasn't any food worth eating in my house because I didn't go shopping when I was away working with my truck.

To my surprise, she called Markson and told him to do just that.

It was about seven o'clock when we heard feet on the porch and then a knock on the door because the bell doesn't work. Steponkus was watching a baseball pre-game show on the TV and she jumped up like she'd been bit.

"Stay there," she said, to keep me on the couch. She drew her gun and slid over to the door. "I heard one. Did you hear one?"

"One what?"

"One person."

But before I could answer there was knocking again and Markson called out, "Open the damn door before this chicken goes cold, Steph. And put the damn gun away." He was smiling big and pleased with himself when Steponkus opened the door and had her gun out like he guessed.

It was a big bucket of chicken. I went and got some plates from the kitchen along with paper towels. That's how Kelly and I eat KFC. You'd never guess from the small size of her that she eats just about as much as me.

"What's the game?" Markson said, and when I got back he was sitting on the couch where I usually sit.

"Cubs in St. Louis," Steponkus said as I gave her a plate.

"A cop's gotta eat what a cop's gotta eat," Markson said, dipping into the bucket. "What do you think, Steph? Take the cuffs off this felon we're hanging out with?"

"Why not?" Steponkus stared at the box.

"Come here," Markson said and he took my cuffs off.

It made a lot of difference to making me feel freer and more comfortable. "Thanks," I said, even though it was an obvious thing for them to do because where was I going to run away to? I was already home.

In the top of the second, Steponkus said, "Did you hear something?"

Markson and I both said, "What?" at the same time.

Steponkus fumbled around for the remote. Markson stood up. Some of his chicken spilled off his plate onto the floor.

When the sound was mute, Steponkus said, "I thought I heard something outside." She stood up too and opened the flap of her holster. "It wasn't loud. Oh, wait."

"What?" Markson said.

"Prince's lawyer said she'd come over here when she could."

"Her? What the hell for? She want to make sure we don't charge him for getting grease on his own damn shirt?"

Then we all heard noise at the door, like someone trying to get in.

"OK," Steponkus said. She pulled her gun out. Markson did too.

Then we heard the sound of fiddling with the lock. A minute later the door opened and it was Kelly.

"Kell!" I shouted and I was so excited that I ran over to her and put my arms around her. "You're safe!"

"Joe?" she said. "Of course I'm safe. But, how can you be here?"

101

"I've been so worried."

"Worried about what? And who are these people? And guns? And chicken? Are you having some kind of party?"

"No no," I said.

Steponkus and Markson put their guns away and Steponkus got a badge out. "We're detectives, ma'am. I'm Sergeant Steponkus and this is Detective Markson."

But Kelly was rubbing her head. I could tell it all happened too fast for her to understand.

Steponkus said, "You would be Ms. Bishop?"

"Of course she is," I said. "But, Kell, where's Little Joe?"

"Joe's in the car for a minute while I set things up for him. But Joseph, what are you doing here? Did they let you go? And if they let you go, why are there cops?"

"First things first, ma'am," Steponkus said. "Go bring your little boy in. Detective Markson will help you with any bags and whatnot."

Kelly pulled tight into my arms It was about the best feeling I could think of. But then she said, "Joe?" and I knew she was getting scared.

"Get the stuff like she says, Kell. We can talk about it all once you and Little Joe are safe inside."

I saw that she heard the word "safe" again, but that probably made up her mind to go to her car for Little Joe.

While Kelly and Markson were out of the house, Steponkus said, "Do you think your lady friend knows about her mother?"

"No," I said. "If she knew, she'd of said."

"Will she want to go to the hospital?"

"Yeah, I'm sure."

Steponkus thought for a minute.

I said, "At least we know Chuckie doesn't have her."

"Yeah. But I'll want your friend to have police protection

until we know what's what with Gardner. If he is after her, he might look for her at the hospital if he didn't get this address from the mother."

I thought about Chuckie at the hospital and I didn't like that at all.

In a minute Kelly was back with Little Joe in her arms I was so glad to see Little Joe after all this time I almost cried. I could tell Kelly could tell, too, when she saw how I held him and kissed his little face, which was asleep.

And I was so glad the handcuffs were off me. I would of hated to hold my boy after all this time with handcuffs on. Kelly already saw me in them, and that was bad enough.

Little Joe's chubby cheeks felt so soft and his little face—

"Joe? Joe?"

It was Steponkus. "What?" I said.

"We're not here for old home week. Do you want to tell Ms. Bishop or shall I?"

"Tell me what?" Kelly asked.

"What?" I asked. Then I remembered.

"Tell me what, Joe?"

"Your mom's in the hospital, Kell."

"Momma's where?"

"She got hit on the head, and they think Chuckie did it."

Kelly's mouth opened wide, and so did her eyes.

Steponkus stepped in and said what hospital it was, and that a cop was with her there. "I imagine your first thought is to go to your mother."

"Yes," Kelly said. "Yes. I want to be with Momma."

"She is unconscious, ma'am," Steponkus said, "and I'll get a call as soon as she wakes up. So before you go anywhere, I really do need to talk to you about Charles Gardner."

Kelly stood there thinking, not knowing what to do. "What

about Chuckie?"

"You saw him a few days ago with George Wayne."

"Yeah . . ." She turned to me.

"I told them what you said. And told them Chuckie's dog was like a German shepherd, you said."

"What dog? Oh, Chuckie's dog?" Then she got it. "And there was a dog with George's body." She turned back to Steponkus and Markson. "You think it was Chuckie's dog? You think Chuckie killed George? That's what you think?"

"We're exploring it as a real possibility," Markson said, "especially if the dog we found with the body is the same one you saw with Mr. Gardner. The problem is, we don't know for sure yet. The dog we have in custody doesn't have a collar or an identification implant. So we may need you to look at the dog and tell us if you think it could be the same one you saw in Gardner's car."

"You want me to look at a dog?"

"Yes, ma'am," Markson said.

"Ms. Bishop," Steponkus said, "do you happen to know where we could find Mr. Gardner now?"

"How would I know that?"

"Mr. Prince says he followed you to your mother's apartment building."

"That was to make sure George didn't . . . Well, . . . Did Joe tell you what George did to me?"

"He made unwelcome advances, yes."

Kelly made a screwed-up face like a bad smell and a bad taste all at once, remembering George's stinky tongue.

"But since then, have you seen Mr. Gardner?"

"No."

"Or heard from him?"

"No. But why would I? I hadn't seen Chuckie for years and years before the other day and it was never like we were friends.

That was him and Joe and George and the others till Joe wised up and left them behind." She turned to me. "Except when they come back into his life and get him into trouble."

She was thinking of George and the time a couple of years ago. And now this time. What could I say? She was right.

To me Kelly said, "Do you think Chuckie killed George?"

"Well, I didn't do it."

"If Mr. Gardner did murder Mr. Wayne," Steponkus said, "then he may consider you a dangerous witness, Ms. Bishop."

"Me?"

"You saw them together. And you saw this dog. And if he does consider you a threat then he may well have attacked your mother and started the fire in her kitchen."

"Fire? What fire?" Kelly turned to me. "Joe?"

"There was a fire, too, but they put it out."

Kelly shook her head a bunch of quick little shakes. "I don't understand about any of this, but I can't think about it till I see Momma." And she took Little Joe back out of my arms

"Ms. Bishop," Steponkus said, "there's really nothing you can do at the hospital."

Little Joe began to cry. "Shit," Kelly said. She looked around. "I'm going to need his stuff." She nodded to a bag that was by Markson because he brought it in.

Markson looked down, then picked up the bag.

Steponkus said, "If you insist, then we're going to come to the hospital with you."

And just then somebody knocked on the door.

"Who the hell is that, Joe?" Kelly asked.

"Just what we need," Markson said. "The fucking lawyer."

So I went to the door, and I opened it. And there was Chuckie.

9

"Joseph?" Chuckie said.

And I saw it in his eyes, that it was all true. He murdered George and set the fire at Freda's and he was here to murder Kelly.

Also I saw that he saw other people behind me. I don't know what they were doing. Whatever it was, it made him turn around and run.

And I ran after him. I never thought about it for a minute first. I just did it.

Chuckie about flew down the path to the sidewalk and turned left, which was the long way down the block but in the direction of Virginia Avenue, the main street nearby. He ran all-out fast at first, looking behind a couple of times to see if I was following or maybe somebody else instead.

I ran fast enough to make sure that I knew where he was, even if I wasn't catching up. If we'd of been in the old neighborhood he might of got away from me by knowing alleys and shortcuts because it was so long since I lived back there. But this was my neighborhood.

I've had this same little house more than ten years, from about the time I got my truck after my lotto win and started earning regular money. I only rent it, but it's a part of town I really know now. In fact, one of the reasons that Kelly and I got back together for good after her bad divorce was because my house is away from the old neighborhood and the guys in the gang.

Kelly and I knew each other a lot longer than we were together full-time, and she never liked it that I got in trouble a lot. Or that even from those first days I had my problem with women when she left me alone. That's what broke us up more than once before this last time. But now we had Little Joe, which was all the difference.

When Chuckie turned the corner he shouted something back at me. I didn't hear what. Only by the time I turned the corner too, I wondered if catching him was what I really wanted. I was never the big fighter of the gang when we were in high school. Chuckie wasn't the biggest fighter either. Probably that was Max, for getting in the most fights, but when Chuckie did fight, he would most often go crazy with it and need to be stopped not to kill somebody.

When he got to Virginia Avenue he ran straight across it and was lucky there were no cars. On the other side he nearly knocked down some guy who was coming out of Skip's Market.

I thought maybe Chuckie would cut down Buchanan or Woodlawn and maybe go for the big berm to the Interstate junction and get mixed up in all of that crossing the lanes with the big trucks. That's what I would of done.

Instead, Chuckie just ran down Virginia Avenue, heading toward the bridge over the Interstate and the city downtown. Maybe his idea was to get lost in all of that, but after only a couple of blocks I saw him turn into an alley just past the White Castle building, where they administrate for their restaurants. That was when I knew I had him.

At night, that alley is fenced off and locked up. It's all wire fence, but it's a dead end. If Chuckie climbed up the fence, which was already about ten feet tall, all he'd find at the top was nasty razor-wire. Truth is, it's a place I know about because in my past I took one or two girls there before Little Joe came along and when there wasn't anywhere much else to go and the weather was good. I'm not proud of it.

I didn't think Chuckie would take his chance with the razors, compared to fighting me. But what I still didn't know was if he had a gun or a knife, or if what he had was just himself, like I did. But since he came to my house planning to kill Kelly, chances were he had something.

When I got to the turn into the little alley, I saw he wasn't even trying to get over the fence. He was too tired. He was just standing there, leaning, and breathing hard. Trapped.

I started walking to where he was. I was breathing too, but not as much as him.

Chuckie said, "Don't make me kill you, Joe."

"Kill me? Why would you do that?"

"It'd be self-defense." He held up a little, shiny gun that I could see from reflections off it from security lights in the yard behind him.

"What defense?"

"No closer." I was about ten feet away from him and he lifted the gun up higher, so I stopped where I was. I could see how he was still out of breath. He was just about breathed out.

And then he let himself slide down the fence so he was sitting at the foot of it. "Fuck," he said. He didn't try to stand up again, but he still kept the gun pointed at me.

"Are you OK, Chuckie?"

"No closer." His talk was in little short bursts with breaks between them. "I'll shoot you." A breath. "I will."

"Why would you shoot me?"

"Why'd you, chase me?"

"Why'd you run?"

"I just came by, for a visit. You chased me, out of the door. Cause . . . cause . . . Cause you thought . . . You thought I was, moving on Kelly. While you were away. Take my chance."

"That's not what you came to my house for, Chuckie."

"I know," he said. "I know. But you didn't know. And you've always, been a hothead, a crazy fuck."

"That's you, the crazy fuck. Not me."

"Yeah," he said. "You right. You right. I'm too tired to make up anybody else, though." And he began to laugh.

I took a step.

"No!" He lifted the gun up again from where it had sagged to. "I will shoot you, Joe. They don't know that, I'm the hothead. I'll tell 'em . . . I'll tell 'em . . . I'll tell 'em I came to see you."

"You didn't know I was there."

"No. You right. But . . . maybe I heard it, about you being released, that's it. On the TV or the radio."

"They didn't release me. I'm not released."

"You're not?"

"They took me back to my house, but I'm still in custody. They only took the handcuffs off so I could eat my KFC."

"Fuck. My story's fucked."

"Yeah."

"But if you're in custody, how come you're here?"

"I told you."

"No, I mean, here. In this." He waved around the alley.

"I ran after you. I never thought about it."

"So you escaped."

"Well . . ."

"You escapee. They'll roast your ass."

I scratched my head. Would they roast my ass for trying to catch Chuckie for them? Or would they think it was me just trying to get away?

109

Chuckie said, "They'll go downtown, and tell 'em you got away, a murder suspect, and it'll be their nuts in the cracker." He laughed some more and he was feeling better. "Murder suspect escapes. You could be front page."

"That's not how it was," I said.

"Try telling them that. Try getting them to say any different."

And I saw what he was saying, how it could look real bad for Steponkus and Markson because they took my cuffs off and now I got away. I could see how that could turn them into crazy fucks as far as I was concerned. Any cop can be a crazy fuck if you cross them.

And if they were pissed with me, then maybe they'd do things to convict me no matter what I didn't do. And then I'd be away from Kelly and Little Joe no matter that all I did was try to catch Chuckie for them. I shook my head.

I didn't know what I should do for the best. Go back and give myself up, so they didn't get so angry? But what about Chuckie? That would leave him at large, and now he knew they were after him.

Or did he? But I wasn't going to ask Chuckie if he knew about the cops thinking he killed George.

The other thing I could do was try to capture Chuckie even with his gun and bring him back. That way they'd know for sure it wasn't that I was trying to escape.

"OK. OK," Chuckie was saying when I saw him again. "I got my story straight now. I did come to your place cause I wanted to jump Kelly. That's it. I knew you were away, and I was always hot for her from the old days. And then, to my shock, you open the door, even though you're supposed to be in fucking jail. Well, of course I ain't going to stick around. I'm going to high-tail it like a jackrabbit. And that's what I did. Yet here you are. About to pound my ass. So that's why it's self-defense."

I found a bit of fence of my own that made an "L" with his

fence. I slid down it and sat on the ground too. "Were you always hot for Kelly from the old days?"

Chuckie laughed, and I began to remember that for all he was a crazy fuck sometimes, he could laugh at stuff. That was always how he was, and I knew him all the way from grade school. "Naa, not my type, Joe."

"I thought they were all your type."

"Too much mouth on her, your Kelly. And not in the good way."

"She don't let stuff slide by, that's for sure."

Now he was feeling better, Chuckie felt around in his shirt and pulled out a pack of cigs. "Want one?"

"I don't anymore."

"Big, bad Kelly won't let you smoke, huh?" He laughed again.

"Go on. Give me one," I said. I slid a little closer with my hand out.

He pointed the gun. "Back, Joe."

I went back.

He took a second cigarette from the pack and lit them both in his mouth. Then he held one out to me, but the gun was always there in his other hand. I leaned in to take it, but slid back to where I was before. "This OK?" I said.

He didn't say, but I could tell it was. What he did say, "Have you noticed how in movies and TV anymore if they smoke they're going to be the bad guys?"

"You think?"

"Used to be the blond guys, and before that the foreign ones, and before that the black hats. But now it's cigs." He drew hard and blew some rings that I could see from the security lights.

I took a little puff, but it made me cough.

Chuckie laughed. "Got you whipped. But I guess you like it."

"I guess. Yeah, I do like it. I love her."

He didn't say anything to that and looked off into the sky.

I said, "Have you got anybody these days?"

"Sure."

"Yeah?"

"Cute little number, does what she's told. I get whatever I need, no problem."

"That's good."

"And if I don't, then I can get all that money can buy." He laughed some more, and smoked. "Damn sight better than being told what to do and what not to do and when not to do it."

I could of told him it wasn't like that, but I said, "And you have plenty of money?"

He fixed me in the eye then, and switched the gun to his other hand. "What are you asking, Joe?"

"Nothing. Just if you make enough money. However. Whatever."

"Not, by any chance, asking what me and George were up to?"

"If it was with George, it wasn't going to be straight. But it's nothing to do with me. Well, it wasn't."

He blew more smoke. "It was George's idea to involve you, Joe."

"Yeah?"

"Use your truck instead of stealing one. Put you out on that damn houseboat of his."

So it *was* gone when I found it wasn't there. I *knew* it.

Chuckie said, "Gave him a kick, cause of how you nearly got screwed the last time you did something with him."

"I did get screwed. Two grand's fine worth of screwed."

"But you didn't go down."

"No."

"And it's only money." He laughed. "Yep, on-ly mon-ey. Always plenty of that around, if you know where to look."

I could of told him it wasn't my money that I got screwed

with, and that made it worse, but I didn't want to.

Chuckie said, "I do think George had it in mind to try for Kelly again, once he saw her. I think he would have too if . . . You know."

"If he was still alive?"

"And if you two were still broke up. All of that."

"Kelly would never ever of gone with George. She hated the ground he walked on."

"Didn't mean he wouldn't have tried, especially if she was home alone. He tried pretty much whatever came into his head, George."

"I guess."

"She was in there today, wasn't she, in the house, your Kelly? Didn't I see that?"

"Yeah," I said. "She was there. But only temporary. Picking up some stuff."

"Oh yeah? And who were the others?"

For a minute I wondered if I should say it was Kelly's brother and sister. But I already told Chuckie about the handcuffs and the KFC. "They were cops."

"Both of them? Or were there more than two that I didn't see?"

"Just the two."

"And they were there looking for me?"

"They were waiting for Kelly," I said.

"Oh yeah?"

"Her mom got hurt this afternoon and she didn't know about it yet. They brought me out cause I was the only one who knew where she might be. It was my hunch she was coming home and it turned out I was right. She only just got there, and we were about to go to the hospital."

"They brought you out, and then bought you chicken? Where'd you find cops like that?"

"They wanted the KFC for themselves. I only got some cause I was there."

"So, what happened to the mom?" He looked cool and casual.

"She got hurt on the head. Lucky it wasn't someplace that might do damage, the old witch."

"She OK?"

"I never got that far to find out how she is, though I do know she never woke up yet."

He thought some. "Not looking for me, then, the cops?"

I was ready for that one. "Do you think they would of let me answer the door if they were there to look for you?"

"Mmm." I saw in his face he could see the sense of that. Course, truth is, Steponkus and Markson only let me answer the door because they thought it was Cayenne.

"You're not smoking, Joe," Chuckie said.

I looked at the cigarette in my hand. It was only just about still alight. "I forgot it." I drew on it till it glowed again. That made me think of the fire in Kelly's mom's house, and of Chuckie setting it with Freda lying there on the floor. I don't like the old witch any more than she likes me, but I still wouldn't of wanted that to happen to her.

I drew on the cig, deeper. I said, "That's good."

"So what you going to do now, Joe?"

"What do you mean?"

"You going to let me walk away?"

"How can I stop you?"

"You can't. Not without I shoot you."

"So there's your answer," I said.

"But what stops you running to the nearest phone?"

"I'll stay here. Long as you say."

"Like hide'n'seek, huh? Count to a hundred?"

"A thousand if you want."

He looked at me. I tried to look like I meant it. He said,

"Ever been shot, Joe?"

"Nope. And I don't want to start now, thanks very much."

"Well, I don't specially want to shoot you."

"I'm glad to hear it."

"So maybe I can work out how not to do it."

"Well, I sure hope you can." I was also still trying to figure a way I could jump him without it being suicide, but he was being real careful so far. The eye of his gun barrel kept me in its sights all of the time.

He said, "I didn't want to shoot George, either."

"No?"

"But he's a twisted fuck, George. Always was. He was trying to screw me out of some money, just because he was holding it. Can you believe that? Old friends like us and he goes and skims some and tries to hide it."

"Not smart to do that to you, Chuckie," I said.

"He knows that now, rest his soul."

"I got no need to stop you doing anything you want, Chuckie. Like walking out of here, no looking back."

"Well, I think that too. I think to myself, What's in it for Joe to give me trouble? He says he'll count to a thousand or a million, why wouldn't he do it?"

"I can count to a million, I bet."

"And yet, Joe, and yet the thing is, you chased after me in the first place. Why'd you do that, Joe? What'd you go and do that for? Why didn't you just say 'Hi Chuckie, bye Chuckie, see you sometime Chuckie,' and turn back into your house and that fine woman of yours and those two cops that feed you chicken?"

"I don't know. I just did it."

"It's a problem working that out, Joe."

"Maybe I figured I could bum a cigarette off you."

He could of laughed at that, but he didn't.

I took another drag. I said, "Kelly came home, so we're made up and I got her and Little Joe again. I don't need to do anything with you."

"No? So if you go back, what you will you tell them about why you ran?"

I opened my mouth but it wasn't clear to me anymore what to say.

He said, "You got your family back, so you didn't need to run out of the house to find them. And you say they're all you really want, so you didn't need to run to escape from the cops either. And yet you still ran after me."

There was nothing I could say to that because it was true.

He said, "And now you want me to believe it wasn't because you were trying to catch me for the cops. Get your story straight, Joe."

I could tell by the way his voice was rising, and his excitement, that this might be the last story I would ever get to tell.

If you're with a woman, and you want her, what you have to do is make her believe she is what you want more than anybody or anything in the whole wide world. Not just that you want her to use, but that you want her, the whole package, every little bit.

To get her, you don't have to be great looking and somebody she pretty much wants already, though it doesn't hurt. But you do have to look at her so she knows she's all you see, and she's all you hear, and she's all you're thinking about. You've got to look at her with a look in your eye that says all that. And if you do that, then pretty soon she's feeling pretty and smart and funny and sexy all at once, like maybe she's never felt it before. She's getting the attention from you that she never got from any other man she can remember at the minute. No matter what she's had at the hands of other men, she feels like at this second she's the queen of the world, and there's a chance, just a chance, it might be real this time.

That's how I think about it when I want a woman. I look at her in the eyes as deep inside her head as I want to be deep inside her someplace else. But to make her believe all that, I have to believe it all too, and what happens is that, for the minute, it becomes true.

And I knew when I was there with Chuckie and trying to answer why I ran after him, I knew I had to make him feel what I make a woman feel. I had to put my whole soul into getting him to want to believe me, just this one more time.

I said, "Chuckie, truth is, I chased you because you ran away."

"Now what kind of reason is that?"

"It was like when we were kids and when we were about to get caught doing something and we ran for it. All it took was for one of us to look up and run, and we'd all run, even if we didn't know what from. That's what I did today."

Chuckie tapped another cigarette out of his pack.

"Truth is, there's a part of me that wants to run away from Kelly and Little Joe, that wants to leave behind taking orders and having to bring home money and hearing about it over and over and over when I make a mistake. Being with someone a long time is a whole lot harder work than it ever is finding somebody new every day or two."

Chuckie lit his cigarette.

"Sure, a part of me wanted to catch up with you and try my luck at beating the shit out of you, because of what you and George did to land me in jail again. But truth is, the truth is, I didn't think about any of that. Not till later. I opened the door and you were there and then you ran, so I ran too. And maybe it doesn't make much of a story, but if you let me go here without killing me, then maybe I'll just keep on running some more. I don't know. I guess I'll work it out then, if I get the chance."

Chuckie sat there, smoking his cigarette. In between drags he

117

took it out of his mouth and rubbed his own lips. He never looked away from my eyes. And now I really wanted another cigarette myself, but I didn't want to ask.

When he did finish his cig he flicked the butt away through the fence and he got up to his feet. Then he said, "Stand up, Joe."

I stood up, being careful not to look like I was getting set to try to rush him for the gun.

He said, "I never thought I'd ever say this, but right now I really wish I had me a pair of handcuffs."

"Yeah?"

And then he shot me.

It might seem that what I said to Chuckie there in the alley didn't work, but I think it did.

If Chuckie'd been a girl in a bar with a drink or two then, truth is, he'd of been going home with me or me with her. I think that because Chuckie only shot me in the thigh. When it was George, he shot him in the head.

Not that being shot in the thigh didn't hurt a lot and break the bone, because it did. But it was his way of not killing me. And after he shot me I was still awake to see him go to the end of the alley. I saw him turn in the direction that was back the way we came.

That got me scared again, even more than I hurt. I figured he was heading back to the house to shoot Kelly after all.

So I tried to follow to stop him.

It was only later I worked out that he wouldn't of turned that way to kill Kelly. He'd of remembered she had cops with her. So he must of gone that way because that's where his car was. Steponkus and Markson might even of driven right past the car, or Chuckie himself, when they came out to look for me.

And I wouldn't of saved Kelly anyway. Because I only got as far as the main street before I passed out in the doorway of the White Castle building. It turned out that Steponkus saw me there when she was cruising the neighborhood to look for where I ran to. She saw me and called an ambulance.

10

What all happened next at the hospital was a kind of blur, all a mix of Steponkus looming above doctors in white jackets and other strangers. Everybody asked me questions. What's your name? Does this hurt, Joe? Who shot you? Do you know your blood type? Are you allergic to penicillin? Was it Charles Gardner at the door? Can you feel this? This? This?

Ow! Damn right I can feel that!

It seemed to take forever, and everybody was there except the one person I wanted to see there. And there were questions, questions, and more questions, no matter how much I answered as well as I could. Yes, it was Chuckie at the door. Ow. Yes, Chuckie shot me. Ow. Yes, he told me he killed George. Ow. No, I don't know where he went. Ow! Please, can I see Kelly now? Ow. Ow. Ow.

And then I stopped remembering anything.

When I woke up again in the hospital I didn't know what day it was or what time. I only knew that Kelly was there with me.

"Kell?" I said. "Is that you?"

"Just about. So, you're awake."

"I guess. My head, though . . ." I felt all blurry.

"You're going to be OK, Joe," she said. "Don't worry."

"Worry?" I tried to sit up and look around, but I couldn't manage that, either. And something rattled. I didn't understand. I lay back down. "What happened?"

"They operated on you in the middle of the night."

"They did?"

"It was to put the bone in your leg back together with pins, including the big pieces that broke off. They say it all went well and you'll be fine in the end. They say it's a good thing you're in such good condition and your bones are strong."

I tried to take it all in. Pieces of bone? I was going to ask some more, but I think maybe I fell asleep because when I saw Kelly again she was in a different chair.

She looked tired. I said, "Hi."

"You're back again?"

"You look tired, Kell."

"Thanks a lot."

"But good. I didn't mean you don't look good."

"I'm not getting much sleep. They've . . ."

"What?" She twitched her shoulder to mean she wasn't sure she should tell me. But I said, "Come on. What?"

"Little Joe and I are in a hotel."

"Not at home? You're not leaving me again, are you?"

"The cops put us there. It's in case Chuckie comes back to the house."

Chuckie. Oh yeah. "He might hurt you."

"They don't think he will."

"I think he will. I mean, he wants to. That's why he came to the house in the first place, even if he tells a different story."

She shrugged and looked tired again. "Either way, they put us in this hotel. I guess it's cheaper than keeping a cop with us all the time."

"So, is it OK there, at the hotel?"

"It's all in one room. If Little Joe goes to sleep it's hard to watch the TV and not wake him up. And they don't like us going out in case Chuckie sees us."

"Oh."

121

"But it would be all right, I guess, if I didn't have you and Momma to worry about. At least you're in the same hospital."

"We are?" Then I remembered about what happened to her mom. "How is she?"

"Still unconscious."

"I'm sorry, Kell."

"Thanks."

I tried to sit up then, to give her a hug. But I hurt too much, and then I saw that what rattled before were handcuffs that locked me to the bed by one of my wrists. "What the hell is this?"

"You're in custody, Joe."

"I am? Even though Chuckie shot me?"

"I think they want to keep you around till they catch him."

"Oh." Even so, how could they lock me to a bed after I got shot? I rattled the handcuffs.

"Please don't do that. You'll wake up Little Joe."

"Little Joe? Where is he?"

"Over by the door. They don't let me bring the stroller up close to your bed. They don't want me to smuggle stuff to you."

A snuggle sounded great. I was tired, but not that tired. I wanted to tell her. But when I opened my eyes again she was gone.

There was a lot of that for a while. Only instead of Kelly it mostly seemed to be Steponkus that was there until I fell asleep, except when it was Markson or a nurse. And it was always the same, Steponkus asking me about Chuckie and what he said and if there was a clue to where he might be or what he did with George.

I told everything the best I could, because there was nothing I wanted more than Chuckie in jail. But a lot of it always seemed to be the same questions all the time over and over. And I also kept going back to sleep again after I woke up. I guess they had me on drugs to keep me tired.

But then the next morning, the day after I first woke up, it wasn't Steponkus that was there to see me but Cayenne. "Hey, Joe," she said. "How you doin'?" She looked full of the energy I still didn't feel.

"OK, I guess. Except for I hurt." And it wasn't just my leg. Other places hurt too. And my head kept on feeling like it was not my own one.

"Well, I have some news that should drive all your pains away."

"What news?"

"They caught Charles Gardner last night."

I looked at her. "For real?"

"He's in custody at IPD even as we speak."

"Yes!" That news did make me feel better. A lot better, because Chuckie behind bars meant he couldn't find Kelly and shoot her. I was about as relieved as you can get. I rattled the handcuffs and laughed. "So it's about to be over at last."

"One step at a time, Joe. But it is a big one."

"How did they catch him?"

"He was driving in Speedway and a cop noticed one of his brake lights was out. It's a cliché, I know. Gardner changed the license plate on his car, but he never checked his bulbs. Then when the cop tried to pull him over, he floored it. The cop called for help and it took five cars to corner him, but when Gardner surrendered he said that when he heard the siren he just ran for it without thinking first."

"He said that?"

"Yup."

I guess what I said to him in the alley helped him pick that story to get straight. "So has Chuckie confessed to the murder of George?"

"No. Unfortunately."

"But he told me he did it to George."

"A lot of things have happened since they caught him, Joe."

I wasn't sure I liked "a lot of things." "Like what?"

"Gardner denies everything except driving with a brake light out. He even says it wasn't him who changed the plate on his car. And he certainly denies shooting George Wayne. He says if you say he admitted that, it's just you trying to get out of the murder you're accused of. He also denies shooting you."

"But he did shoot me."

"He says he was never even in the little alley where you were shot. He says someone else must have done it."

"But that's plain crazy."

"He also says he came to the door of your house expecting to find Kelly alone."

"That part's true. He wanted to shoot her. He had a gun on him to do it with."

"His version is that when they ran into each other last week Kelly invited him to come over sometime, because you and she had broken up."

"I only wish now I had a gun of my own for when he came to the door." Chuckie really made me mad with all these lies.

"Nobody believes him, Joe. I'm just telling you his story. He says he was surprised when you opened the door instead of Kelly. And that's why he ran. But he says he outran you and that he has no idea where you went or how you got shot."

I rattled my handcuffs. "What about his gun? Won't a bullet from it match what they took out of my leg?"

"There was no gun on him or in the car when he was arrested."

"What about at where he lives?"

"He says he doesn't have a place of his own. That he's only

124

passing through town and has been sleeping in the car."

"That can't be right, with Kelly seeing him more than a week ago. Even if he didn't have his own place he'd of stayed with somebody."

"The only person we know he had contact with was George Wayne and the police didn't find any of Gardner's fingerprints at the houseboat."

Just mine. It made me sad to think of all the trouble I wouldn't of had if only I didn't take the deal for three hundred dollars from George in the first place.

"Joe, do you have any idea who Gardner might have stayed with?"

"I haven't even heard about Chuckie for years. He used to have a mother, but she was dead by the time we got to high school." Then I remembered, "He did say he had some woman."

"Who?"

"All he said was she was a cute little number that did what he told her to."

"Charming." Cayenne wrote something in a notebook. "When you were in the alley with Gardner, Joe, did he say what he'd been up to with Wayne?"

More of the same questions, but at least this time they were from Cayenne. I shook my head. "Not more than that they took my truck."

"Well, do you remember that on the day I met you at IPD I said I'd look through the crime records for those that overlapped the time you were on the houseboat?"

"I remember that."

"There were plenty of crimes to choose from, but the standouts were five house burglaries near Geist Reservoir and none like them before or after the days you were on the boat."

"That's got to be Chuckie and George."

"I did locate the burgled houses on a map and at least four of them must be visible from where the houseboat is—and the fifth may be. It's farther from the shore, but higher up, so maybe there's a clear sight line."

"He had field glasses out there."

"All the houses were empty when the burglars struck, though some had alarms and/or surveillance cameras. The tapes the police have looked at show two men, but they masked their faces and nothing shows the vehicle they were using. The two men were in and out quickly at each place. They took small antiques, jewelry, laptop computers, and whatever cash they could find. The police say the insurance claims will be something like twenty or twenty-five thousand dollars, though of course the bad guys wouldn't have been able to fence what they stole for anything like that. Nevertheless, they'd have come away with well into four figures."

"So there was nothing about my truck?"

"One police interview turned up a neighbor who remembered a white truck—though no plate or make or distinguishing marks. But another neighbor thought he'd seen a blue van—which could have been there for something legitimate, of course. There've been almost nothing else in the way of witness reports so far."

I shook my head. I was so mad at George all over again for setting me up that I could hardly think.

But then Cayenne said, "Joe, there's something else. There was another cluster of robberies that all took place on the first and second days you were on the boat. Again, two men—with their faces covered and wearing hats. They robbed four gas stations and convenience stores of their cash. All the places they hit sold lotto tickets—I don't know if you know it, but there was a twenty-two-million-dollar rollover draw while you were on the boat, so all these places were doing a lot of business. Altogether the two guys scooped about seven grand in cash. And twice witnesses said they saw the robbers run to a white truck."

"That's got to of been Chuckie and George too," I said. "In the old days they both liked robbing gas stations better than the rest of us. They liked how they always got free candy with it."

"Now that's interesting," she said.

"What?"

"When Gardner was arrested they found a box of candy bars in his car." She wrote more stuff in her book.

While she did it, I suddenly got an idea. It was that Chuckie didn't kill George for skimming money like he said. I bet Chuckie killed George to get it all. They'd of fenced the stuff they stole from houses fast so it wouldn't be hanging around. Say they got a few thousand dollars for it all. Ten or twelve grand is a whole lot more than five or six. Plus there was the roll of cash George carried on himself. I said, "How much money did Chuckie have on him?"

"A couple of hundred dollars."

"If that's all he was carrying then he's got the rest hidden someplace."

Cayenne wrote some more before she said, "When his picture was in the paper and on TV I don't think anybody called in about where he was staying, but I'll ask Steponkus."

"So what's happening to Chuckie now," I asked, "if he didn't confess and they didn't find his gun?"

"They're holding him on suspicion of shooting you."

"Did they do that test on him they did on my hands for if I fired a gun?"

"I'll check. Although after a couple of days there's not much chance of it showing anything. All it takes is a good wash."

"He did shoot me, Cayenne."

"I know he did, Joe."

"And he was in that alley by White Castle. In fact, I just thought of something else."

"What?"

"He smoked two cigarettes and threw the butts away. Can't they get his DNA off those, or his fingerprints? Didn't I see that on a TV program once? That would prove he was there."

"I'll tell Steponkus about the butts." She wrote something down. "Because our problem is that, so far, there just isn't any hard evidence to contradict Gardner's story."

"They're not going to let him go after all of this, are they, Cayenne?"

"Not if we can help it."

"Because he did shoot George, as well as me."

"That's something else I want to talk to you about, Joe. Getting a kind of evidence about George Wayne's murder."

"What evidence?"

"If you agree, I want to take you over to IPD this afternoon."

"What for?"

"So you can be part of an ID parade for the dog. Your doctor says it's OK if we're gentle with you, and bring you straight back."

I didn't get at first why the ID parade had to have me in it at all. Who the dog might identify was Chuckie, from being his dog and because she was in his car. But the reason for me to be there was that Chuckie's free lawyer tried to stop a dog ID parade altogether.

The lawyer said parades were only meant for people witnesses, not for dog witnesses. So what, if the dog wagged her tail at Chuckie? What did it prove except maybe that Chuckie smelled like dogfood?

But the police went to get a judge to make Chuckie be a part of the parade. And this time the judge was a smart one, and she ruled that Chuckie had to take part. Let the jury decide what it means, she said, and she ruled there had to be a video of the dog doing its ID as well.

But then the lawyer said "Why just Chuckie? Prince was the one out on the boat," so the judge said if Chuckie's lawyer wanted the dog to smell me too, then fine.

But it wasn't easy to set it all up. It turns out a dog ID parade is more than just lining a bunch of guys up and walking a dog past them. It turns out it matters who is walking the dog. A dog can be influenced by who holds the leash. The judge looked it all up and said there was research done on the dogs that sniff out bombs and drugs.

Like, if the guy walking the dog sees somebody that looks suspicious to him then sometimes the dog can tell through the leash and it will bark and jump like it smells something even if it doesn't.

That can be OK for drugs and bombs because then when they search the guy they can find out what isn't there and let him go. But in a case like this, if the witness dog wags her tail and licks Chuckie's hand there's no way for a second double-check on it.

So the judge told the cops they had to find somebody to walk the witness dog that was experienced with dogs but didn't know anything about Chuckie or about me or the case. And it all took time to set up, and they were doing it even while Cayenne was with me in the hospital. And it took more time for the nurses to work out the best way for me go to the IPD.

In the end they put me in a wheelchair with my leg sticking out straight in front of me and I rode with Cayenne and a cop in an ambulance.

In the IPD they rolled me to an elevator and took me up to one of the rooms they have for interviews. I was there about twenty minutes with Cayenne and the cop when I realized I had a problem.

I said, "How long is it before the parade?"

Cayenne said, "They have to clear a room, get the equipment set up, and bring Gardner down from the lockup. They'll call us when they're ready."

"Truth is, Cayenne," I said, "I really need to go to the bathroom."

"Oh, Joe. Can't it wait?"

"I don't think it can." In the hospital it was set up to be easy for me to do when I was still in the bed. But I didn't do that with Cayenne there and when I got excited about going to the IPD then I kind of forgot about it. Till now.

"Wait here." She went out and left me with the cop standing guard against me escaping.

I asked him, "How far to the men's room?"

"Not far. Turn right out the door, the elevators are a little way along. Once past them, take the first corridor on the left and you're there."

So at least I knew where it was for when Cayenne came back, which wasn't more than a couple of minutes.

"It's OK, Joe," she said. "But they insist that an officer goes in there with you." She turned to the cop.

"I'm Vablitzky, Miss. I'm happy to accompany the prisoner."

"I'll come along too and stand outside, Officer Vablitzky," Cayenne said, "and it's Ms."

"Got it, Miss Ms." Then he held up his hands. "Just funnin', ma'am."

Cayenne held the door and Officer Vablitzky rolled me out and turned me to the right. About the last thing I expected to see in front of me was the back of a guy walking a dog. And it was *the* dog, too, because it was a German shepherd.

"Hang on," Cayenne said.

But she didn't have time for Vablitzky to turn my wheelchair back into the interview room so the dog didn't see me. What happened was that in front of the dog Chuckie got off the elevator and turned our way.

Chuckie was in handcuffs with a cop and when he saw the dog was near to him and coming his way he stopped where he was.

The dog stopped too, and she crouched down and she growled and then she began to bark.

When she did that Chuckie raised his hands up, to protect his face in case the dog jumped at him to bite. But when Chuckie did that, the dog jumped backwards, like she was afraid he was going to hit her.

11

It turned out that the screw-up of the whole ID parade was because the witness dog had to take a leak—like me. But the dog expert didn't know he was supposed to ask anybody. He just saw the dog had to go, because he was an expert, so he took her down the corridor towards the elevators in order to take her out. He didn't think about maybe they'd be bringing Chuckie on an elevator too.

When the cops heard the dog barking they ran out into the corridor from everywhere. It seemed like they were all shouting and calling names at the same time.

What came out of it was that now the whole ID parade was off, because Chuckie wasn't an equal stranger for the witness dog like everybody else anymore. Cayenne sent me back to the hospital with Vablitzky while she stayed at IPD to fight out what was going to happen next.

I nearly died in the ambulance, from having to piss. I only just made it to the hospital without doing it right there on my cast. I would of hated that, because the cast was all white. It would of showed up for everyone to know, like pissing in the snow.

And then I got handcuffed to the bed again. Vablitzky stayed in the hall outside my room till another cop came to replace him. I would of been jumping up and down to know if what happened with the witness dog meant Chuckie was going to get away with it after all, if I wasn't so tired and full of headache myself. But then Kelly came in pushing her stroller with Little Joe asleep in it. That freshed me right up.

She left the stroller and her purse by the door. I don't know if Steponkus had the ambulance bring me to the same hospital as Kelly's mom on purpose, but it sure was a convenient thing.

"Hey, Joe," Kelly said when she sat down.

"Hi, honey."

"You feel OK?"

"Not bad. They had me out of here and over at the IPD."

"I know. I came up before."

So her mom must be on a lower floor somewhere. "So how is she?"

"About the same. They say it's good she's breathing on her own, but it's bad she hasn't waked up yet."

"I hope she gets better," I said. "I do. Honest."

"Thanks, Joe."

"You still look tired, Kell."

"What do you expect me to look, with you here and Momma downstairs?"

"I was just saying."

She nodded, and looked tireder yet. "Little Joe's been crying in the nights. That doesn't help."

"Misses his dad, I bet."

"He's teething, Joe. It's not all about you." Then she shook her head like she was sorry and she took my hand.

I took her hand back but I did it with the one that was farther away from her. I didn't want to hold hands with my one that was handcuffed. "Are you and Little Joe still at the hotel?"

"Not since they got Chuckie in custody. He isn't a danger to us anymore, so they took us back to the house because Momma's place isn't fit to live in."

"Would you of gone back to your mom's instead, Kell?"

"I wouldn't want to, but I might of." She shook her head

again. "I don't know where my life is going right now. But I do know that I just can't be going through all of what you put me through over and over again, Joe. Especially not with Little Joe getting bigger."

"I don't want you to go over and over it, Kell," I said. "I've been working on my problem, I really have. I've been overcoming myself and growing up. I'm better. I really am. When I look at Cayenne and Steponkus, I don't feel a thing for them. I only feel for you."

"Just who the hell are Cayenne and Steponkus again?"

"My free lawyer, and the cop that arrested me."

"You've got the hots for your lawyer and your cop?"

"I didn't. I don't. That's what I was saying. I've been days and days without you. Way more than a week or ten days, now. And I don't feel it like I used to. And I know in my heart, over and over again, that it's you I want and nobody else."

"How about the cute nurses, Joe? How about the volunteers who bring the magazines around? And the gals who serve your food?"

"That's what I'm saying. I'm really trying this time. And I'm going to be better. I already am."

"And what I'm saying is why the hell is it so damn hard for you?"

"I don't know, Kell. I never did."

"It's not like you're fifteen anymore. And it's not like I'm a kid either." She took her hand away. "Right now it all just makes me tired, Joe."

"Please," I said. "I love you, Kell."

"I know." She stood up. "For what it's worth."

"Don't leave me."

"I want to get back before Little Joe wakes up."

"I mean don't leave me. Not again. Not now. Not ever."

"We'll talk, Joe. When this is all over."

"But you'll be there? You'll be at home?"

She walked to where Little Joe's stroller was and looked into it and smiled. "Yeah," she said. "I'll be home." Then she left.

Even if she was only back because she couldn't go to her mom's, I was still so glad she was back that I about cried. I remembered how I felt when she left me that last time. I hated it. And it really wasn't for days and days that I had the urge in me to be with anybody instead of Kelly herself. Not really. And truth is, right then I was about too tired to have the urge for Kelly herself.

I slept.

In the night after dinner I had two more visitors. Cayenne and Steponkus. It was funny seeing them together at the same time, the one so little and the other so big. But before they came into the room they talked a while to the cop outside my door. And I got worried.

What if despite everything—despite the dog and what Kelly saw and Chuckie coming to my house and shooting me—what if the cops let Chuckie go? And what if they decided to stick with what they had against me in the first place, which was fingerprints on the shotgun. What if they put me in front of a judge and it was a bad one, and the judge convicted me so that I never got to see Kelly and Little Joe again. What if—

"Joe? Joe?" Cayenne said.

"Oh. Sorry," I said. "But tell me now. Is it bad that it's the two of you? Because I never did murder George and that's the honest truth."

"Relax, Mr. Prince," Sergeant Steponkus said.

"We bear glad tidings, Joe," Cayenne said.

"Pretty glad," Steponkus said.

"You're being released."

"What?" I said.

"But there are conditions," Steponkus said. "You're not to leave town without our permission. And if you move to a different address, I'll need to know where, so I can find you if I need to."

"They may still want you as a witness, Joe. But they're not going to charge you with George's murder."

"At this time," Steponkus said.

"Yeah, yeah," Cayenne said. She turned to Steponkus. "Steph? The honors, please."

Steponkus unlocked my handcuffs and took them off. She also set down a bag she was carrying by my bed. "These are your belongings, Mr. Prince. If you'd just sign this receipt . . ." She gave me a pen and a piece of paper and showed me where to sign, so I did.

Then I rubbed my wrist that had been locked up so long. And all of a sudden I began to cry. "Does this mean I can go home?" And I cried some more before I stopped.

"The doctors say it isn't safe for you to leave here yet, Joe," Cayenne said. "It may be several more days, but as soon as they give the OK, you're free to leave."

"I want to go now."

"When the bone is messed up like yours was, there are chances of complications. You need to be here so if something goes wrong it can be treated immediately. It's not just a matter of making it more likely that you'll be able to walk right again. Things could go wrong that would even threaten your life if they weren't treated quickly."

"From just a leg?"

"The bullet hit the bone, Joe. But ask your doctor about it."

I said, "OK," but I didn't really feel it. I was just tired again.

"When you get the all-clear, Mr. Prince," Steponkus said, "we'll set it up for you to be taken home by ambulance."

"So you finally believe me now that Chuckie shot me, and

that he killed George, and he hit Kelly's mom on the head and he set her apartment on fire?"

"I believe those things, Mr. Prince. And while we investigate we are continuing to hold him on suspicion."

"Just on the suspicion?"

"We simply don't have enough hard evidence to arrest Gardner yet."

"Can't we do the dog ID parade again another day?"

"Unfortunately," Steponkus said, "the fact that the dog came face to face with Gardner in the hallway today makes another ID parade impossible."

"But," Cayenne said, "it may work out that we wouldn't need another one anyway. We spent time with the judge this afternoon talking it through."

"We certainly did," Steponkus said.

"She was not happy about what happened," Cayenne said. "But she has accepted that it was an honest mistake, so she's allowing us to take statements from the people involved, and she'll allow them to be called as witnesses if it comes to a trial."

"Nobody asked me to state anything," I said.

"The important witness is the dog handler, Mr. Tejeda," Steponkus said. "He convinced Judge Marsh that he had no idea who any of the people in the hallway were."

"And he's also sure from the way the dog behaved that she did have prior knowledge of the man he later found to be Charles Gardner," Cayenne said.

"So the expert says the dog already knew Chuckie?" I asked.

"Yes."

"So that proves Chuckie shot George, right?"

"It's certainly a link in the chain of evidence against Gardner," Cayenne said, "but they'll need a lot more links before the chain is strong enough to put him away."

It seemed pretty clear to me, except at the minute nothing

seemed all that clear to me, because of how I was so tired.

Cayenne said, "Mr. Tejeda also told the judge that the dog's behavior suggests she associates Gardner with serious trauma of some kind."

Steponkus said, "The dog was bleeding from the shoulder when we took her off the houseboat. The vet at the dog pound removed shotgun pellets from her shoulder. The pellets are the same type as those found in George Wayne's head."

"Chuckie shot the dog?" I said.

"The theory," Cayenne said, "is that maybe when Gardner shot George Wayne the dog was near the line of fire. Mr. Tejeda says that the noise of a shotgun blast, plus the pain of a wound could easily have upset the dog so much that she wouldn't allow Gardner to take her off the houseboat when he left. And that would explain how she came to be there."

"That's the theory," Steponkus said.

"But Kelly saw the dog with Chuckie and the dog ended up on the boat. How else would it get there if Chuckie didn't take it in the first place?"

"It is a connection that supports the theory," Cayenne said.

"Well, it all seems obvious to me," I said. "I don't know what more you need to lock Chuckie up and throw away the key."

"It will take more for a jury, Joe, believe me."

"So what about you, Mr. Prince?" Steponkus asked.

"What about me?"

"Do you remember anything else that might help us prove that Gardner shot you, or that he shot George Wayne?"

Cayenne said, "Steph, maybe you should run through what's already been done."

"Did you find Chuckie's cigarette butts?" I said.

"We gathered about fifty smoked cigarettes from the site," Steponkus said. "But our lab people say that rain we had two days ago means there won't be any DNA or fingerprints left on any of them."

"Tell him about the security tapes," Cayenne said.

"We're going with the idea that Wayne and Gardner committed the Geist area burglaries, and maybe the lotto-cash stickups as well. So we've hired an expert to look at the security tapes taken from the burgled houses and lotto-cash robberies. He'll measure up fixed points at the crime scenes and use them to calculate the heights and body shapes of the masked gunmen. The idea is to compare what he comes up with measurements we take from Wayne's body and from Gardner. We may be able to prove the same men did both kinds of crime, and that those men are Wayne and Gardner. And it's possible he'll come up with other things, too, once he's studied all six tapes."

I frowned. "I thought they did five houses and four lottos."

"Unfortunately, Mr. Prince, not all the premises had working surveillance equipment."

"It's still a lot of crimes to do in three days and get away."

"Makes you wonder where the police were during all that, doesn't it?" Cayenne said. "I wonder if we'd see a spike in Krispy Kreme sales figures."

"Anybody tell you about the spike in murders last week?" Steponkus said.

I said, "But if I know Chuckie and George, they would of planned it out before they began, so they knew where to go and what order to do them in."

Cayenne looked at Steponkus. "Steph, have you looked at tapes from earlier in the week, especially from the lotto places?"

"Not so far," Steponkus said. "But I see what you're getting at. If Gardner or Wayne checked out places ahead of time, they might show up on tape, and not in disguise. I'll look into it."

I said, "What about the candy box in Chuckie's car?"

"The candy the lotto-robbers took does include some of the same brand we found in Gardner's car," Steponkus said. "But there's nothing on that box to prove it came from a particular store."

"However it is another bit of circumstantial evidence," Cayenne said.

"As for the assault on Mrs. Kovic and the fire at her apartment, we've also had officers question the neighbors, but so far nobody remembers a man asking about Mrs. Kovic or her daughter."

"Maybe somebody saw the dog," I said.

"Would Gardner have taken it around with him?" Cayenne asked.

"What I mean is he could of left it in his car. Somebody parking there might of seen a green Ford with a dog in it."

"Steph?"

"I'll send somebody around the building again."

"And did you find where Chuckie lives yet?"

"No. The addresses on his license and car registration are out of date and we haven't had any useful responses from the public yet."

"How about the guy coming out of Skip's Market?"

"What guy?" Cayenne said.

"When I was chasing Chuckie, he ran across Virginia Avenue and knocked into a guy that was coming out of Skip's."

"Did you mention this before, Mr. Prince?" Steponkus asked.

"I don't remember. But I didn't know I was going to have to prove Chuckie shot me more than having his bullet in my leg."

"Go on, Joe," Cayenne said.

"Well, just about everybody that shops at Skip's lives in the neighborhood so you ought to be able to find him to ID Chuckie."

Steponkus wrote something down.

My head was hurting, but still I said, "The guy outside might even of seen me chasing after Chuckie, too. I was only on the other side of the street, and that would prove that Chuckie didn't lose me when he tried to run away, cause it's only just a couple of blocks from Skip's to the White Castle."

Both Cayenne and Steponkus wrote in their notebooks. It made me feel good, like I was maybe helping.

"Anything else, Mr. Prince?" Steponkus said.

"I'll keep thinking on it."

Steponkus stood up. "OK. I'm outta here. Maybe see if I can find a guy who buys his food at Skip's Market." She left, waving a hand, only it was more like a paw it was so big.

Before Cayenne said anything then, I asked her, "Do you know how Kelly's mom is now? Because if she wakes up she's another witness who could tell you that Chuckie did it to her."

"I'll check Mrs. Kovic's condition on my way out. If there's been a change, I'll come back and let you know."

"Thanks."

"So, Joe, do you want me to call Kelly to let her know you're a free man?"

"I'd rather do that myself. Only my room doesn't have a phone."

"That's because the police are covering your medical bill and they don't want you calling China."

"But I don't know anybody in China."

She stood up. "I'll ask a nurse about a phone you can use if you want to do it now."

"Thanks."

She said, "We did it, Joe. We got you out of those cuffs." She smiled and looked me in the eyes.

And I didn't feel a thing. I really didn't.

Once Cayenne was gone the first thing I did was to look in my bag that I signed for before I was too tired. And it was all there, four hundred and thirty-six dollars, just like went into it in the

141

first place. That made me believe that everything was about true. I was free again. I rubbed my wrist.

And I was going to go home, to live with Kelly and Little Joe, once I was better and could walk again and wouldn't die from things going wrong. And I was going to be grown up now, I really would, and I wouldn't give Kelly her worries anymore about leaving me alone, though I hoped she wouldn't. I never liked it when Kelly left me alone.

"Joe? Joe?"

"What?" It was a nurse who came in, one I knew, Rob.

"I didn't realize you were asleep. The lady said you want to make a phone call."

I showed him my wrist. "I'm free again."

"Congratulations."

"So I want to call Kelly and tell her I'm coming home."

"You won't be leaving just yet, Joe."

"I know." But then, what I wanted more than anything was to go home and do it right now anyway, because Kelly would be there and I missed her so bad.

I saw in Rob's face that he saw in my face what I was thinking.

"It's just not safe yet, Joe," he said. "You wouldn't want to get home and then have an emergency and have to come back. Or maybe not be able to get back in time."

I didn't say anything. I wanted to go home. That was my emergency.

Rob set me up in a wheelchair to roll to the phone the nurses have. It was a lot closer than the public one and it was only a local call, not China.

But when I dialed at first I thought I was going to get the voicemail, only then Kelly answered just in time.

"Kell?"

"Joe? Is that you? Is something wrong? Has something happened to Momma?"

"It's nothing wrong, honey. It's something right. I'm a free man again. Steponkus took my handcuff off and took away the cop at the door."

"Oh, Joe, that's wonderful."

"I miss you so bad, Kell."

She didn't say anything for a minute then.

"What I want more than anything is to come home now." When she still didn't say anything, I said, "Kell?"

"Are they discharging you, Joe? Is that it?"

I didn't want to tell Kelly a lie. "No."

"They don't want you to leave yet?"

"There's little chance I might get complicated and have to come back. But they took me out to the IPD already today and nothing bad happened. So I figure I can come home now and it'll be OK."

"I don't think you should leave if they don't say you're ready, Joe."

"Don't you miss me?"

"Of course I miss you. And I do love you, Joe."

"I'm really glad when I hear that."

"That's not the problem. It never has been."

"I'm better. I mean I'm good. I'm really really being different."

"It's not always just about you, Joe. Over and over you act as if what you want, what you need, is the only thing that should matter to me. Well, Little Joe matters to me too. And my momma."

"I didn't forget about your mom, Kell. She's the same. Cayenne would of come back to tell me if she changed."

"I could also use a little time on my own right now."

"Oh." I didn't like the sound of Kelly having time on her own.

"And if the doctors think it's better for you to stay in the hospital, then I think you should stay."

It's not what I wanted to happen. I know what I want isn't the only thing in town all the time, but right now I really wanted to come back home and be with Kell.

"And if you are different now, Joe, then you won't mind waiting a little."

"I still hate being alone from you. That's not different."

"I know."

That was really hard to hear, the tone in her voice. And I was just too tired to fight it anymore.

"Joe?"

"OK. I'll stay. It wouldn't be good for an emergency to happen and me to have to come back here. You've got enough to look after and everything now already."

"I think it's the right decision."

"OK."

"And I will see you tomorrow."

"OK."

"It really is best, Joe."

"OK."

She took a pause, because she wasn't going to get me to say it was what I wanted. Then she said, "See you tomorrow," and hung up.

Rob was there and he could see how disappointed I was, even though he tried not to look like he was listening.

I said, "I better go back to my bed now."

Rob wheeled me back to my bed and helped me get in. Only despite I was really really tired I still didn't go to sleep right away. Here I was, a free man, but because of what Chuckie did to me by shooting me I was stuck here in the hospital instead of being home with Kelly again.

If I didn't have the shot leg I could help her with Little Joe and look after him while she visited her mom. And if I was at home with her, right there in the room with her and holding her hands and having a couple of beers, I bet I could of made her happy to have me there again. I always did before.

Only instead of being with Kelly, I was in the hospital. Alone.

I felt it really really bad alone.

For a while I even wondered if my wheelchair would go down to one of the wards where they had women. Maybe Rob would take me.

But I didn't try to do it. I didn't ask.

And I didn't want to. Not really. What I wanted was to be with Kelly, only she was there and I was here.

12

I kept waking up in the night because my leg hurt. In the middle there was a new nurse taking Rob's place and she was Dinah. She put a new bag of painkiller on a drip and then she sat with me for a while before she had to leave and look after somebody else.

She told me how broken legs from bullets are worse than other broken legs because of the shock waves in addition to what the bullet hits. And then she told me about her boyfriend, Boyce, and how bad he was treating her and she didn't deserve it and he'd be sorry when she was gone.

Dinah was young, quite a new nurse, and with a nice face, yellow hair and a nurse-hat that was greeny and looked good in the hair. She had blue eyes, too, big blue eyes, and after a while talking to her it seemed like her nurse-hat would change colors from different angles of looking. Sometimes it was good with her hair, but other times it was good with the color of her eyes.

"I really like your hat," I said.

"Do you?"

"How do you get it to change its colors like that?" I asked her.

"It's a special material. Haven't you seen it before?"

"Nope."

"Oh I bet you have. Just maybe not in a hat. It's the same as they have on some of those Volkswagen Jettas, only there it's blue but sometimes it changes to purple in a different light."

"Oh, you mean like the Jetta George had?"

"Exactly. See, Joe? I told you you'd seen it somewhere before." And she smiled a big smile.

But then I got the feeling something was wrong. "Dinah," I said, "how come you know about George?"

"I don't. Not really. All I know about him is enough to hate him."

"You do?"

"You know I hate him, Joe. I hate how he makes passes at me when you're not there, but I hate most how he always gets you into trouble."

And then Dinah moved a little bit, and in the different light she changed into Kelly.

"Kell? Is that you?"

"It better not be anybody else, Joe."

And I would of been so perfectly happy for it to stay just me and Kelly together, and to let nature take its course, only I woke up. And a few minutes later they served me breakfast.

After breakfast I didn't feel like I'd slept much. There was something itchy in my cast but I also felt antsy in myself. It reminded me how I felt on the houseboat after the first day—except on the boat I didn't have a broken leg, of course. And on the houseboat at least I could go out to the deck to look at the *Sunbird*.

But in the hospital I had to lie there and just get fed up with it all. I had the TV, but who cared? I just didn't know what to do with myself. Kelly would come to see me today but I never knew when. And maybe the doctor would come in and say I was all healed enough to go home, if Kelly didn't mind it. But even knowing stuff would happen in the future still didn't make it better for me now.

After a while of itching and twitching I called for the nurse with my button. This time she wasn't one I already knew, but her badge said she was Linda. I asked her when the doctor was coming because I wanted to go home.

"The doctors get here when they get here," she said. And she didn't smile or act friendly or anything at all except being in a hurry.

Finally at about eleven I did have a visitor at last, only it wasn't Kelly or the doctor. It was Cayenne, and that surprised me because I wasn't even sure she was still my lawyer if I was a free man.

"How you feeling today, Joe?" she asked.

"I want to get out of here."

"I'm not surprised." She sat down and I heard her do a sigh.

"What?" I said.

"I really thought we were about finished with your case, Joe. But there's been a development."

"What development?" It couldn't be good from the way she was saying it.

"Charles Gardner has come up with an alibi witness."

"What witness?"

"A woman presented herself at IPD first thing this morning. She says Gardner was with her the day five of the nine robberies were committed, including three of the four lottos. And she also says he was with her for the whole of the night George Wayne was murdered."

"But that's crazy. Chuckie was with George to shoot him. He told me so, and he also left the dog there."

"That's the other thing."

"What other thing?"

"The woman says she owns a dog. Care to guess what breed?"

"I don't want to guess."

"A German shepherd. And she says that her boyfriend,

Charles Gardner, looks after her German shepherd dog sometimes. He often takes 'Maisie' with him in his car, especially on days when she has to go to work, which is as a waitress at the Denny's on Thirtieth Street."

"I don't believe any of that," I said. "Except maybe the waitress part."

"Steph Steponkus is, shall we say, skeptical of her story. But she has to take it seriously enough to check it out."

"But what about how the witness dog from the boat already knew Chuckie yesterday?"

"Gardner's lawyer argues that the houseboat dog was barking and aggressive when she was recovered in the first place. So when she barked at Gardner yesterday it needn't mean anything more than that the dog just picks people to bark at sometimes."

"But that's not what the dog expert said. And he's an expert."

"And I believe him. However, the new circumstances may undermine his testimony. It's quite a normal defense strategy to offer an alternate theory."

"I like the first theory."

"It'll be for the police and the DA and a judge to work it all out, Joe. I very much doubt that they'll come back and accuse you of Wayne's murder. Nevertheless, we have to be prepared. Which is why it is still my case."

"It all sounds stupid to me," I said. "How can they think again I shot George after I got shot?"

"It helps that you got shot, Joe."

"It doesn't help me much," and wouldn't you know it? Just then I got this horrible great big itch in my leg that I couldn't get anywhere close to. I just had to bang on my cast.

"It helps in the sense that Steponkus knows personally you didn't have a gun when you left your house to chase Gardner. She watched you long enough to believe you didn't pick one up from a hiding place along the way. She's sure Gardner shot you, even if she can't prove it yet."

It was all too dumb and crazy even to think about. I just rubbed my face hard, like I wished I could scratch my leg under the cast.

"There's something else, Joe."

I didn't say "What?" this time because so far all the whats turned out to be bad.

"Gardner's lawyer is pushing for him to be released."

"Released? They can't do that. He killed George and he shot me and he bashed Kelly's mom on the head."

"The lawyer says now there's an alibi witness the police have less evidence to hold his client with than there was against you. And since they've let you go . . ." Cayenne shrugged both her hands out. "It all comes down to the evidence, Joe. Steponkus will hold Gardner as long as she can, but Gardner's lawyer is seeing Judge Marsh this afternoon and I'm sure she'll release him if his alibi stands up."

"The alibi woman is lying. Can't they see that?"

"They're checking her story even as we speak." Cayenne looked in her notebook. "The woman's name is Emily Tuck. Is it familiar at all?"

"No."

"Tuck says that Gardner didn't tell the police about her in the first place because he wanted to protect her reputation."

"Chuckie? Protect somebody not himself? That's just a joke that's not worth laughing."

"The police will do their best to break the alibi, but I wanted you to know the score. They won't be able to keep Gardner in jail for driving a car with a faulty brake light or the wrong license plate or failure to update the addresses on his paperwork."

I tried to think about that. "So he might really get out?"

"It is possible."

"But he shot me. And he would of shot Kelly. And he already

cracked Freda on the head and tried to kill her with the fire."

"Calm down, Joe." Cayenne patted my hand that wasn't cuffed anymore.

"Joseph, what's this?"

The voice was from the doorway and it was Kelly, here in my room with Little Joe. "Hi, honey."

"Just who is this . . . woman?"

And right away I could tell she was remembering all over the time she caught me being flagrant with the redhead.

Cayenne stood up and said, "You must be Kelly."

"You got that right."

"Well, I'm Joe's lawyer, Kelly. Cayenne Davenport." And she put out her hand.

Kelly came farther into the room, and I could see she was thinking stuff, but she didn't say any of it and just shook Cayenne's hand. "I thought the police released Joe and he didn't need a lawyer anymore."

"He has been released but there was an unexpected development this morning. I stopped by to tell Joe because he is still technically considered to be a suspect."

"How can he be a suspect? Chuckie shot him."

"Chuckie's gone and got someone to lie an alibi for him," I said. "Cayenne says they might even be going to release him now."

"But that's crazy," Kelly said.

"That's what I said."

"It's not just he shot Joe. He broke open my Momma's head and set her house on fire." Kelly was getting upset about it like I did.

"Unfortunately," Cayenne said, "the police can't prove those things, yet."

"And he would have killed me too, Joe says. Jesus! How can they release him? What's wrong with everybody? If Chuckie's out he'll kill us all."

"I don't think he'd do that anymore, Kell," I said. I was really upset to see how upset about it she was, but I didn't say it just to make her feel better. "Chuckie would of killed you so you didn't tell about the dog and how you saw him with George. But you've already told it now, so killing you wouldn't help him anymore."

I really wished that I could jump up out of my bed and put my arms around her for comfort. But then Cayenne must of felt the same thing because she said, "I know it must seem like the police aren't getting anywhere, but they will." And she went over to Kelly and hugged her and Kelly let her.

Cayenne said, "Police resources are stretched thin because of other crimes right now, but I know for a fact that Sergeant Steponkus badly wants to crack this case. She's just been thrown off track a bit by this new witness showing up with a possible alibi."

"And what's more," I said, "the alibi witness bought a dog, too."

"What dog?" Kelly asked.

"The alibi witness says the dog you saw with Chuckie was her one, not the houseboat one."

Kelly looked confused.

Cayenne said, "Kelly, might you be able to pick out the dog you saw from a group of German shepherds?"

"Not in a million years. I didn't look much at the dog with Chuckie. I just saw it was there and the kind it was." She frowned. "But can't they tell one dog from another from the hairs it left behind in Chuckie's car?"

I didn't say anything for a minute, because I wished I'd thought of that.

Cayenne wrote something down. "I'll ask Steponkus if she's checking that. I don't know if IPD's forensic lab is geared up to do canine DNA comparisons from hair. But differences between the dogs might show up on visual comparison anyway."

"The only thing I thought of," I said, because I just did, "is that the witness woman must of bought her dog someplace in the last day or two since she only found out she needed one after they caught Chuckie. Maybe the cops can find out where she bought it from and prove that."

"That's good too, Joe," Cayenne said. She wrote some more.

And then somebody at the door talked to us all and said, "If I'd known you were having a party I'd have brought some Cape Cods."

We all turned and there was a woman in the doorway in a white jacket. "I'm Doctor Jepson. Sorry to break up the shindig, but I need some time alone with Mr. Prince now."

Kelly went off to visit her mom on the fourth floor and Cayenne said she'd call Steponkus with Kelly and my ideas once she was outside and allowed to use her cell phone. And then I was alone with the doctor.

"How are you feeling today, Mr. Prince?" she asked.

"I'm feeling like I want to go home now."

"And I'd love to send you home now. But it ain't gonna happen. Not for a day or three."

"Why not?"

"Ever heard of blood clots?"

It turned out that my risk of that and infections was elevated and I needed medicine and observation. The doctor also wanted me to see a physiotherapist while I was still here, so I could learn how to be on crutches when I finally got the chance. "You look like a smart guy to me, Mr. Prince," she said, "so I'm not going to ask anyone to teach you how to sit in a wheelchair."

"I was in a wheelchair already," I said. "They took me in it to the IPD and back yesterday."

"Oh yes?" She looked at her notes and wrote something. "Well, you're ahead of the game then. I'll get someone to bring you a chair. But be careful while you're still learning to steer it with that leg sticking out."

"It sounds like driving a truck, and allowing for how it's not like a car anymore."

"You drive a truck?"

"I move things for people in it. It's how I make a living for Kelly and Little Joe."

She nodded while she looked at her notes. "Now . . . Has anybody talked with you about how long it may be before you're walking again without crutches?"

"No." I didn't like the sound of how long.

"Or that you may, possibly, always have a bit of a limp?"

"Nobody said that to me."

"It all depends on exactly how the bone heals, and I'd say that chances are you'll probably be fine. But it's a bad break, Mr. Prince. Don't think it isn't."

"I don't think it isn't."

"And a lot of how well you recover will depend on how well you listen to your doctors . . . And how well you do what we tell you. It's not like listening to politicians, where if they say one thing you know you'll be better off doing the opposite."

"I won't do the opposite."

"Good." She got ready to go. "I'll get the paperwork for the physiotherapy started now. The sessions will probably need to continue for quite a long time after you've gone home. But with any luck at all, we'll end up with you as good as new."

Good enough to work would be good enough. Lying in the hospital wasn't going to feed my family. And then I remembered the money I hadn't given to Kelly or told her about. She ought to have it as soon as she could, because I didn't know how much money she had left of her own.

"Wait, wait," I said, but the doctor was already gone.

I was going to ring the button for a nurse, but Doctor Jepson must of read my mind because she came back with a nurse, who was still Linda, the nurse who was in a hurry with me when I called her before. "Set Mr. Prince up with a wheelchair, will you?"

"Yes, doctor."

"He should spend as much time in it as he's comfortable with, once he gets used to moving to it from the bed and back. If you could help him with that to start . . ."

"Of course, doctor," Linda said.

"Just don't push yourself, Mr. Prince, eager though you may be," Doctor Jepson said. "If your leg hurts, listen to it. Time spent in bed helps you to heal too."

When the doctor left again, Linda stayed. "She spent a long time with you."

"Did she?"

"Usually it's three minutes and move on to the next."

"I guess being shot isn't what she gets every day instead of being sick."

"Maybe. Shall I get that wheelchair for you now, Joe?"

And I was surprised she even knew my name because when she came in the first time she wasn't friendly at all. "Yes, please," I said.

I didn't have to wait long. Linda came back with a chair and she already had it so my broken leg would be supported and stick out.

Then she helped me off the bed and into the chair by showing me one chair arm could go down and how to lock the wheels. I was surprised by how strong she was, but gentle, too. She held herself right up close to me, but probably she had to.

"There you go, Joe," she said, when I was sitting in the chair and ready to take the brakes off.

"Thank you," I said, and I really meant it because now I could get myself around to places which would start with the fourth floor where I hoped Kelly would be with her mom. If Kelly was there I could give her the money, and I bet she'd be glad to have it.

But Linda said, "Now let's get you into bed."

"What?"

"I need to be sure you can do it without falling or hurting your leg."

"Oh."

"Roll yourself over to the door, then come back and position the chair by the bed just the way it is now."

And I did it, and she helped me again, and I got into bed, and it didn't hurt me much.

"How was it for you?" she said.

"Good. I'm sure I can do it for myself now."

"Well remember, if I'm here you won't have to." And then I saw in the look on Linda's face the one I recognized from places like Berringers and from the girlfriend on the *Sunbird*.

But what happened then was a patient who came to my door and said, "Oh, nurse. There you are," so Linda left.

But I started feeling really edgy. With me being a fixed prisoner in my bed at night and not able to go home to Kelly, I could see how I might end up with a hard problem, no matter how much I tried to be strong and grown up. No matter how strong you are, sometimes you're weak. It's just the way life is.

Once I calmed down some, I got out of the bed and into my chair without any help. My plan was to go down to the fourth floor. I found the bag of belongings Steponkus brought back to me and I got the money out.

Even though I wanted to get to Kelly if she was there, first I practiced driving the wheelchair. The funny thing was that if my toe did hit something, which it did the first time I aimed through the door, it wasn't the toe that hurt like holy hell but my leg under the cast. So I listened to it, and went really slow.

But before I got off my own eighth floor, there was Linda again. And she tied a red hanky to my toe to be a warning, like on the back of a truck when stuff is sticking out. I was grateful for that, too, because I could see it would help people not run into me. Which would hurt just as much as me running into them because my leg wouldn't know who started it. But I tried not to look at Linda when I thanked her.

13

Kelly wasn't with her mom when I got to the room.

I told the fourth-floor nurse, Harry, who I was and he remembered Kelly and he said the baby started crying so she decided to take him home where he could sleep better. "She said she'd be back sometime this afternoon," Harry said. "But if you want to sit with Mrs. Kovic for a while, that's cool. You can talk to her."

"Talk to her?"

"People in comas, their brains kind of hear it when people talk to them. It can help them to wake up. It really can. Especially if it's voices they're familiar with, like family."

I looked at the old witch, who still wanted to break me up from Kelly enough to set her up in the training business. "I wouldn't have anything to say."

"Tell her everyday stuff, or recite a poem, or tell her about a TV program you saw last night."

"She doesn't want to know about that."

"It doesn't matter. Tell her anything. Really." And then he left me alone with Freda to answer a visitor at the desk.

Truth is, Kelly's mom wasn't very familiar with my voice because she hated me so much, even though I probably wouldn't of told Harry that because Kelly wouldn't want me to say it to a stranger. But Freda and I almost never talk and we don't meet up for holidays, even though now she has a grandson who lives right here in town, unlike her other one. Take

Christmas, for example. Kelly opened her presents under the tree at our house, and then she had to take Little Joe over to her mom's for a whole nother Christmas.

Or take how I wasn't even invited to the funeral. That was what started off every single thing that happened since. Kelly wouldn't of left me or been at the Kroger in the old neighborhood, and I wouldn't have been in Berringers to meet George. If the old witch had only invited me to the funeral she wouldn't be unconscious in the bed right now.

I wondered if Harry would of told me to tell her that in talking to her. Was that what would wake her up?

Truth is, though, I didn't have anything at all I wanted to say to Kelly's mom that I would say out loud to her. But I also didn't want to go back to the eighth floor where Linda was. And then it occurred to me, if I was the one talking to Freda when she did wake up, then that would help when I talked with Kelly about us getting back together for good.

So I wheeled my chair up close to the bed to give it a try. But Freda did not look great. Still, who does, with half her head bandaged up and dark rings around her eyes and baggies hanging from racks by the bed connected to her arms with plastic pipes?

Before I started, Harry came back. "Can I get you a drink of something? Coffee? Or a pop?"

"A pop would be good. Just nothing diet. Thanks."

"Do talk to her, Joe. Or sing. Or read the phone book. Whatever comes into your mind. Anything. Kelly talks to her all the time. This morning she was telling her about the baby. How he's teething."

"Right," I said, and Harry left again. Only the idea of Kelly telling all about Little Joe to her mom who couldn't even hear it, but not to me, made me sad.

I looked at Kelly's mom again. Truth is, I was getting tired, what with the new thing of being in the wheelchair. But I didn't want to be not talking when Harry brought my coke. So I said, "I don't know why you hate me so much, Freda. There would never be another man who loves Kelly more than me, especially now we've got Little Joe together. I know I wasn't the most reliable guy in the world when I was younger. And I know—I really do know, now probably better than ever before—that I make Kell unhappy sometimes. But I love her, Freda, and I'm trying hard to be better and more grown up, so Kelly won't have another time that makes her want to leave. But let me tell you, even though I try, it can still be a struggle, especially when they get that look in their eyes."

And then I heard a sound behind me, and I saw Harry was leaning against the door. He must of been there listening for a while because he wasn't in the middle of moving, so the pop must not of been very far away to get. He came into the room and gave me a can of grape, and then he left me alone with Freda some more.

But when I turned back to the bed it seemed like I didn't have anything else to say to her. So I just opened the can and watched her breathe for a while. Then I looked around the room. There wasn't much to see at first, until I saw a corner with a couple of toy blocks in it. I knew they were Little Joe's because I made them. I sanded down the edges for hours so he wouldn't hurt himself, even if he put them in his mouth. He must of thrown them from his stroller and Kelly didn't pick them up yet.

Seeing the blocks started me off crying. I just blubbed, keeping as quiet as I could, because I missed Kelly and Little Joe so much and I didn't want to have to explain it all to Harry if he heard.

But the old witch heard. She must of. And if me crying

wouldn't wake her up to celebrate, then nothing else I was going to say would do it.

When I finally stopped myself I began to tell her about the Cubs against the White Sox game I saw on the houseboat. I don't know why I thought of that. But if it didn't matter what I said to her, then it didn't matter.

I told her about how inter-league games were new and it always used to be that American League and National League teams only ever played each other in a World Series. And then I told her about the Black Sox of 1919 who were the White Sox that threw the World Series, except for Shoeless Joe Jackson who was the one honest player. Later, all the other cheating players said so. But he was still banned from the Hall of Fame because of the others, even though he was a great player and deserved the Hall of Fame and played barefoot and hit .408 in 1911 which is still the best ever by a rookie. I used to think of myself as Shoeless Joe Prince sometimes when I was a kid and hitting a ball around a lot with a stick, though I always had sneakers.

Talking about it made me think about how in a way I was like Shoeless Joe now, because he was falsely accused and so was I. And a bit of how I was angry for him became angry for me. I drank some of the grape when I thought of that.

And then a woman came into the room.

She was only about twenty and skinny with brown hair that was tangled when it hung past her shoulders. She was pale, too, but with some blotchy places on her face. I thought she was looking for a nurse and was a patient herself, except she had ordinary clothes on. So I decided maybe it was directions she was looking for.

"Hi," I said. "Can I help you or something?"

"Is this Mrs. Kovic's room?" the woman said. So I knew she

wasn't there by an accident or a patient.

"Yeah," I said. "Do you know her?"

"I'm a neighbor. Well, not right next door or anything, but I heard about how she was in here and I thought, man, that's really awful to have a fire like that. They wouldn't tell me much on the phone, see, cause I'm not a relative. So I decided to come in to see how she was."

"Well, sit down for a bit."

"I don't know . . ."

"Really. Do it. I'd offer you my seat . . ."

And she kind of laughed, because of how I was in the wheelchair. "Yeah. OK. For a minute or two." She brought a normal chair up and sat on the other side of the bed. "How is she? See, I don't even exactly know what happened to her."

"She got hit on the head by a guy named Chuckie and then he set a fire to her kitchen with her lying right there so she would burn."

"No shit." She looked at the bed again and her face showed really shocked. "Did she get burned?"

"No. Just knocked out and into a coma."

"Did she wake up?"

"No, not yet. Harry's telling people to talk to her to help, because inside her brain maybe she can hear it even if she doesn't really know. So I guess that means they think she will wake up eventually."

"Oh. Good."

"I bet even us talking like this across her bed does the same good, because Harry the nurse said it doesn't matter what you say, so it won't matter if we're talking to each other and not really to her, cause inside her brain she won't tell the difference."

"Oh."

"Look, I'm Joe—Kelly's boyfriend and Little Joe's dad. And

you are . . . ?"

"I'm Lee. Glad to meet you." She began to stick her hand out to shake but then she stopped, because it would be across Kelly's mom's body, in fact across her crotch. "Jeez," she said, and we both had a bit of a laugh.

"Lee, can I ask you a question?"

"What question?"

"A few days ago was there a guy in the building that talked to you? I mean, I bet guys talk to you all the time, but I mean one that asked you about Mrs. Kovic and where she lived, and her daughter, Kelly?"

"No. Nobody talked to me like that."

"Or you didn't happen to see a green Ford out back in the parking lot that had a German shepherd dog in it?"

She frowned, maybe because I was asking her funny questions, but she shook her head. "No, I didn't see that either."

Oh well, it was worth a shot.

Then I said, "Do you, like, know Freda—Mrs. Kovic—to talk to in the apartment building?"

"Sure. I see her sometimes, but only to talk to about stuff like when they're going to pick up the trash after holidays and how come there's dirty stuff getting left in the halls so long." She shrugged.

"Well then, I was thinking maybe I could ask you a favor."

"What favor?"

"I want to go back upstairs where I'm a patient here too. And the favor would be for you to sit and talk to Freda for a while. Harry says it's extra good if the person talking to her is one she knows the voice of. So since you talk to her sometimes, that includes you."

Lee looked again at Kelly's mom and I could tell she didn't really want to do it. "I only came in to see how she is, Joe."

"Well, any time you could stay would help. Cause I really

163

ought to get back up to the eighth floor, which is where my own bed is."

"Is that about your leg?"

"Yeah."

"What happened to it?"

"It got shot."

"Shot? Really?"

"The same Chuckie that did this to Freda shot me, too."

"No shit." She looked from my leg to Freda and back again.

"I think he was planning to kill me so I'm not complaining if he only shot me in the leg. But truth is, I'm tired and I also ought to be in my own bed in case the doctor or somebody else comes around. So, would you stay and talk here to Freda for a while?"

"I guess I can stay for a few minutes more."

"That's great. Thanks." I rolled myself toward the door but not before I glanced at Lee's face again and saw how she looked at Kelly's mom as if it was all something kind of creepy.

When I got back to the eighth floor I didn't see Linda at first, so I located my chair next to the bed so I could get myself back in like I learned earlier. What I wanted to do was to take a nap.

But because I was tired, I wasn't as good at getting from the chair to the bed as when I practiced it for Linda. I almost slipped on the floor and only just got myself back into the chair to start over. And because I made some noise doing it I wasn't surprised when Linda was there again at the door to my room. And I was too tired to say, "Let me do it." Truth is, I was glad of a little extra muscle to make it easier.

Again she pressed up close and, truth is, her warm body up tight on mine felt good, but I was too tired to fight it.

Not that anything else happened except she helped me get my covers straight. And she told me I looked tired and not to overdo it. And she said a nap was a good thing and would make me all big and strong again. Then she went off to nurse someplace else. Maybe Linda being there in the afternoon made it more likely that she'd go home, and not be any trouble for me to be more mature in the night anyway.

Then, while I was lying there, I wondered if I did have to fight off the good feeling when Linda's body was up close to mine. Maybe it was like looking at some woman and thinking, "She's fine," but as long as I wasn't touching her or trying to or thinking about her while I was with Kelly, it was still all right to look and appreciate her. Maybe doing that was even a part of how it works when a guy was older and more mature.

The important bit was not doing anything. So maybe when a mature guy has a warm woman press up close to get a better grip, maybe that's OK, as long as he doesn't grab her back.

I didn't know, though, if I would ever get the chance to ask Kelly about it.

"Joe?"

Not without upsetting her or making her think maybe I wanted somebody else when really all I ever wanted was her.

"Joe?"

And it was Kelly, right there by my bed. "Oh, baby."

"You didn't seem like you were really asleep, because of the way you were breathing and kind of talking."

"Was I?"

"But then when I talked, you didn't talk back. So maybe you were asleep."

"Well, maybe I was a little bit asleep."

"I didn't want to wake you up, but I've got to go back home soon."

"I wouldn't want you to go without I saw you, Kell. Seeing you is about the best thing that can happen to me here."

"Well, I'm glad to see you're OK."

"I was in my wheelchair today."

"Was it OK?"

"Sure. And I went down to see if you were with your mom, only Harry said Little Joe needed to go home."

"Yeah, I took him home."

"Where is Little Joe?" Because I didn't see a stroller.

"Harry said he'd look after him in Momma's room for a few minutes. He thinks Little Joe talking to her might be good."

"He told me about talking to her too. I spent a long time down with your mom and talked to her until I got tired."

"That was nice of you, Joe."

She smiled then, and it was a smile with a warm look that I hadn't seen since before she left me. I was really glad to see it again.

"I'll go down there again some more," I said.

"Harry said a woman came in and then you left."

"Yeah. Do you know some neighbor of your mom's called Lee?"

"No."

"Well, she wanted to see how your mom was. I don't know how long she stayed, though."

"Not long, Harry said."

"So is there any change in her condition?"

Kelly shook her head. And I could see then she was getting tears. "I'm scared, Joe. I don't want her to die."

I put my arms out for her to come into them and she did and I held her. "I bet she'll be OK. We just have to keep talking to her."

"I guess."

And we held each other together until she wanted to dab her eyes. When she did from the box by my bed, she said, "Harry said you were crying too."

"I didn't know he saw."

"When all this is done, Joe, when Momma is better, I want us to try to get together and all of us be a real family."

"That sounds good to me, Kell." Especially because it meant her and me being together. Truth is, I bet I could talk for a year to her mom, and be the one who woke her up, but she'd still hate me. But I didn't say that.

"I ought to get Little Joe," Kelly said.

And then I remembered. "Before you go, honey, I've got something here that's just for you."

"Joe, it's a hospital room."

"I mean this." I pulled out the money I took down to her mom's room in the first place. "It's four hundred and thirty-six dollars."

She held it in her two hands like she didn't believe in it. "Where did you get all this?" She looked up. "Joe . . . ?"

"I worked for it. I worked really hard while you were away from me, but I only just got it back because the cops kept it for evidence till they released me from custody. So I want you to have it, because you probably need it already with being back home."

"Thank you, Joe." And this time the look was about how it might not matter it was a hospital room after all. At least that's how it looked to me. Only then Linda came in.

"Mr. Prince," she said, "it's time for supper. Do you want me to bring it in now?"

Kelly got up and said, "Go ahead and eat, honey. See you tomorrow." She kissed me and left.

And even if I had the time I wouldn't of told her that Linda bringing the food in for me herself wasn't the way it was usually done, which was by someone else rolling a cart around.

While Linda set my bed table up she said, "That your girl-friend?"

"Yeah. Kelly."

"She looks nice."

"She is. Very nice."

"Kinda little, though." She said with a smile, because she was pretty big, and then she went out to get my food.

When she came back, I said, "Kelly may be little, but she's very strong."

"You like 'em strong, do you, Joe?"

And I couldn't say no to that, could I?

Linda put the food tray on my table. "Here you go. If you see anything you'd like more of, you just let me know, hear?"

Truth is, once I got eating I would of liked more of the chicken à la king, which was one of my favorites from being a kid when my mom always said it was a dish fit for a Prince. But I didn't ask Linda for more because I didn't want her getting the frame of mind of doing things for me, if you know what I mean.

What I decided instead was to try to remember to ask Kelly to bring extra food if it wasn't too inconvenient. Like maybe some peanut butter. I thought maybe after dinner I could get in my chair again and find a phone to make a call. But I decided first I would give Kelly more time to get home, and also to see if maybe Linda was going to finish with her shift.

So once Linda took the food tray away, I turned on the TV. It was the news, and what it came up to saying was, "Police today released another suspect in the Houseboat Murder Case. We'll have all the details for you when we come back."

Another suspect released? All in a single moment I was upset and mad and confused. How could the cops go and release Chuckie? How could they do that after he murdered George and shot me and injured Freda into a coma?

When the commercials finished, the TV newswoman said some jokey things to her newsman partner and then he talked about a traffic accident on IS70. Finally they came back to Chuckie and in a minute she said, "Channel Five's own Penny Martin is with us live from the courthouse and she has the story."

"Thanks, Gloria," Channel Five's Penny Martin said. "It was only about an hour ago that Detective Sergeant Stephanie Steponkus came to the press room and made a dramatic statement in which she announced the release of Charles Gardner, the latest suspect in the Houseboat Murder Case."

And there was Steponkus talking on the TV. She said stuff like, "Hard evidence is proving difficult to find," and "We still have a lot of leads—almost too many—and we're following them up as fast as we can," and "I'm confident that we will resolve this case with an arrest and a conviction."

After the statement Channel Five's Penny Martin asked Steponkus questions. "Does this mean that both the men who have been held and then released are no longer suspects in the murder of George Wayne?"

"Not at all. It means we don't have enough hard evidence to continue to detain either of them at this time."

"So you hope to re-arrest them once you get more evidence?"

"Anything is possible. It depends on the evidence."

"Do you think they may have worked together? Is that a possibility?"

"It's not really appropriate for me to offer a theory before we've assembled our evidence."

"But you do think one or both of them committed the murder?"

"I didn't say that either. It's entirely possible that neither of these two men was involved, and that it was perpetrated by someone else entirely. We're just going to have to see where the trail of evidence leads us."

And then, after Steponkus, there was a bald guy who turned

out to be Chuckie's lawyer. He said, "I want to congratulate the legal system for finally doing the right thing and releasing my client, Charles Gardner. Considering that he has a rock-solid alibi and that the accusation against him was made by a previous suspect in this case who was trying to deflect attention from himself, you'd be forgiven for thinking—as I do—that Charles should have been released before today. But at least justice has now been done. I do want to say that my client and I both extend our deepest sympathies to the relatives and friends of George Wayne. We earnestly hope that the police will soon find the evidence to put the real perpetrator of this ugly murder behind bars. Meanwhile, however, we shall be considering a lawsuit for false imprisonment of my client."

Then it was Channel Five's Penny Martin who came back on the TV and said, "I'm sure that IPD is giving its best shot to this murder on Geist Reservoir but, if you ask me, so far it looks like the police are headed upstream and may be out of their depth. This is Penny Martin on the steps of the courthouse. Back to you in the studio."

I didn't watch the rest of the news. Or anything else.

Despite everything I said to Steponkus about Chuckie and what he said to me and did to me when we were by the White Castle, and despite all the things she said she was going to check for evidence, she still released him.

And she said that maybe he didn't do it at all.

And she even said, right there on the TV, that I was still not ruled out as a suspect.

I couldn't hardly believe it.

14

Before the news on the TV what I intended was to go off in my chair again after dinner. But hearing about Chuckie being released and me still being a suspect . . . Well, I just stayed in bed, trying my hardest to figure stuff out.

Steponkus talked on the TV about wanting evidence, but there were already so many evidences she could of found. There was the money from the robberies, and the gun, and what the expert said about the witness dog. There was people seeing Chuckie at Kelly's mom's apartment building or in the parking lot. There was the video expert measuring the robbers up for Chuckie and George, and there was even proving dog hairs in Chuckie's green Ford were from the witness dog and not the alibi dog. There was the guy Chuckie ran into outside of Skip's Market. And all of it, *all of it,* still wasn't enough to keep Chuckie in jail, not even counting that he told me himself he killed George.

It was all crazy.

What I wanted most was for Steponkus to show up in my room right now so I could ask her what the hell she was thinking of letting Chuckie go. And saying on the TV that maybe I still did it.

Only instead of Steponkus, the first person to stick her head in after I turned off the TV was Linda. She said, "I've got some extra dessert you can have if you'd like it, Joe."

I shook my head and said, "No."

"Not in the mood?"

But before I could say anything to that I got a real visitor, only it was Cayenne. "I can see by your face that you've heard," she said.

"Yeah."

She pulled up a chair and then looked back to the door where there was still Linda. "I'm Joe's lawyer and we need some privacy, please," Cayenne said, and Linda left.

I said, "I just watched it on the TV."

"Judge Marsh must have gotten up on the wrong side of her bed this morning. Steph Steponkus expected to be able to extend Gardner for another thirty-six hours, but Gardner's lawyer pitched for a release and he got it."

"And Steponkus said I was still a suspect."

"Don't lose heart, Joe. Steph's a good cop and if the evidence is there, she'll get it."

"Meanwhile Chuckie's free and on the loose to do more damage like shooting people and hitting them on the head and setting fires."

"Do you think he's a danger to anyone in particular now?"

"I'll be a danger to him if I ever catch up with him again, even with my leg. I should of made a move for his gun when I had the chance. I might of saved us all this trouble."

"Or you could be dead. From what you told us, I think you acted very wisely, given the circumstances."

Truth is, I think I acted wisely too. Only at the minute anything seemed better than having Chuckie on the loose again. "Maybe," I said.

"Maybe he's a danger, or maybe you acted wisely?"

I thought about if he was a danger. "I don't think he would look for Kelly now. It wouldn't stop her saying what she already told the cops."

"True."

"But I might be wrong. He might want to get revenge on her, and I sure don't like it that he's out and she's at home. Can't the police put her back in a hotel to be safe again?"

Cayenne hesitated about that. "I can ask them, Joe. But I doubt they'll do anything more than tell the patrol cops in the neighborhood to give the house some extra attention."

I got an idea then. "What happened to the witness dog?"

"Well . . . She's still at the pound, I guess."

"If they don't want her as a witness anymore, can Kelly have her? Because at least if the dog is in the house she'd bark and growl if she ever got a sniff of Chuckie and that would warn Kelly."

Cayenne wrote something down. "Would Kelly want the dog there?"

"I can ask her."

"I'll talk to Steponkus and see if it's possible."

"Tonight?"

"It's not going to happen tonight, Joe. I don't know how long it would take."

"Well, do it anyway. Because nobody wants the dog, right? I mean, Chuckie and the alibi woman aren't going to claim her if they say the other dog is their real one, are they?"

"I'll see what I can do."

"Thanks," I said, and I felt better about it, because at least I was doing something for Kelly and Little Joe, even if it couldn't happen right away.

"What do you think about the chance of Gardner being a danger to you, Joe?"

I thought about that. "He's probably sorry he didn't kill me in the first place, but if there was any more harm I could do him by telling things, I'd of already done it. I think he's more likely to run for it."

"I said that. I wanted an order to have him tagged. But Judge

Marsh just wasn't having any. She said, 'The guy has an alibi for the murder. Your main witnesses against him are an ex-con with something to gain, and a dog. Charge Gardner with something else or break down the alibi. Otherwise release him. What's for lunch?' "

"So it was lunchtime he was out?"

"Steponkus still had a couple of hours, and she tried to get the DA to hold him on the traffic charges, but he wouldn't back her up. I think everybody over there is worried about being sued."

"Great."

"Well, from here on, I'll do my best to keep you up-to-date, Joe, but I can't promise to come to the hospital every day."

"So you're not going to be my free lawyer anymore?"

"I am your lawyer, until the case is done. But I do have other cases that need my attention."

"What about Steponkus saying on the TV that maybe I still did it?"

"She doesn't believe that."

"She said it."

"She doesn't believe it, Joe."

"Or that it wasn't Chuckie at all. She said that, too."

"There's a difference between what she'll say on the television and what she really thinks."

"What difference?"

"It's like being a trial lawyer, Joe. In a trial we never want to ask a question if we don't know what the witness's answer will be. Well, a police officer on television isn't going to say anything she can't already prove. At the moment Steph Steponkus can't really prove anything, so she's not going rule any possibility out during a TV interview."

I didn't know what to make of that. Why ask questions if you already know the answers?

"Steph released Charles Gardner because the judge made her do it. But this isn't over, and he hasn't gotten away with it. You really need to take my word for that."

"OK, I guess."

Cayenne got up. "I'll find out about the dog. But is there anything else I can do for you?"

I thought about asking for some peanut butter, but I didn't really care about it anymore.

Once Cayenne was gone, I lay there in my bed looking at the ceiling. I was really tired with everything that happened all day, but I was confused too.

With all the stuff that could tie Chuckie in to the things he did, I didn't understand why Steponkus and the cops didn't get even one of them to pay off.

Right there in the bed I went through them all again, and tried to think of some more.

And I got an idea. If Kelly's mom would only wake up, she could tell the cops that it was Chuckie that bashed her on the head into a coma. She could pick him out of a human ID parade that wouldn't all go wrong because a dog had to pee.

And I realized that if I went down to the fourth floor and talked to Freda a whole lot, then maybe my talking would be what finally woke her up like Harry said. Cause if only she would wake up, then everything would work out.

And again I thought that if I was the one who woke her up, then maybe the old witch would decide she owed me something. Maybe she'd even get off Kelly's back about me, which would sure help me to be a better boyfriend to Kelly and father to Little Joe. Being those two things was about all I ever wanted to be in the world. I missed Kelly so bad . . .

And then I had another visitor in the door.

I couldn't see at first who it was.

Until he stepped into the room. It was Chuckie.

I sat right up. "What are you doing here?"

"Just thought I'd see how you're doing, Joseph, now that I'm free and not in jail."

I tried to look behind him for a nurse, even if it was Linda, because of what I saw in Chuckie's eyes. It was a look of murder.

He held up a finger. At first I thought it was a gun. "I let you live the last time. Don't push your luck."

And I didn't. I put my own finger up on my lips, to show that I wasn't going to shout out for help.

"Good boy," he said. He came over to the bed and sat down.

I tried to lean away, because he still looked scary, but leaning away made my leg hurt.

"Don't be frightened, Joseph," Chuckie said.

"I'm not."

He took out a pack of cigarettes. "Yes you are."

"You're not allowed to smoke in here."

"You going to stop me?"

"No."

Chuckie lit a cigarette and offered it to me.

"No thanks."

"Go on, smoke."

I shook my head.

"I said smoke."

So I took it and inhaled it and it tasted good, kind of minty. "Is it menthol?"

"Yeah. How did you guess?" And he laughed and I figured it was because he thought that any idiot would already know it was menthol, but I didn't.

"I used to smoke these when I was a kid," I said.

"I know. I was a kid too, you know."

"But they'll kill you, in the end."

"What will?"

"Cigarettes."

He laughed at that. Then he jumped at me, only it was a joke. "They won't kill you if I kill you first."

"I thought I wasn't supposed to be frightened."

"I'm not going to kill you, Joe. Not you."

And all of a sudden I realized what he meant. The judge already said my word against his wasn't enough. So of course he wasn't going to kill me. Who he was going to kill was Kelly's mom. She was the danger to him. If she woke up.

When he left me here, he was going to go down to four to make sure Kelly's mom never woke up to convict him.

"Linda!" I called out.

"Shut up, Joseph," Chuckie said.

"Linda!" I called again.

Chuckie's face grew dark and red and angry again. He stood up by the bed.

But I didn't care. I was the only one that could save Kelly's mom and stop Chuckie. "Linda! Linda!"

And then she was there beside me to wake me up.

"Easy, Mr. Prince. Take it easy."

Only it wasn't Linda. It was another nurse.

"Linda's not here," she said. "Her shift's over. I'm here now. I'm Carol."

My heart was pounding away. My leg hurt, only it didn't. Somehow. I looked at Carol.

"Linda will be pleased to hear you were asking for her," Carol said. "And I see what she means about your eyes. They're lovely."

"Was it a dream?"

"Was what a dream?"

"Just now. Chuckie. Was he in here? Did I have a visitor? A man? Or maybe he only just left to go down to the fourth floor."

"No, Mr. Prince. You haven't had any visitors since I came on. Not even a male nurse."

I thought about that.

"Are you all right now? You back with us?"

It was a dream. It wasn't real.

"Are you going to be all right now? Can I leave you alone?"

But the part about Chuckie killing Kelly's mom . . . That was real.

"Mr. Prince?"

Because if I could work out that Kelly's mom was the danger for him to be put in jail then, for sure, Chuckie would work it out too.

"Mr. Prince?"

"What? Oh. Yeah. Hi. You're Carol."

"You scared me there for a moment. Should I get a doctor in just to make sure you're all right?"

"A doctor? No. No, I'm fine. But . . . Yeah, what I want, . . ."

"What?"

"I want my wheelchair."

15

It needed thinking to work it all out, but if I was going to think it was better for me to do it downstairs by Kelly's mom. I told Carol where to bring the wheelchair by the bed and I didn't even suggest for her to help me, and I did it fine by myself and hardly hurt my leg at all.

But when I got down to the fourth floor, it wasn't Harry on as the nurse anymore. The new one was Alison, so I had to explain all over about who I was. But all I said about Kelly's mom was that I wanted to sit by her bed.

"She's unconscious, you know," Alison said.

"Harry who was here before you said that talking to her might wake her up."

Alison made a doubtful face. "Good luck."

Kelly's mom looked about the same when I got into her room. And that was good, because it meant that Chuckie hadn't killed her yet.

And he hadn't tried yet, either, because I went back out to Alison to ask if there'd been other visitors by the bedside tonight, but there hadn't.

But then once I got back by Kelly's mom again I realized something else, and it was that when Chuckie did come in to kill her, I'd have to think of some way to stop him that wasn't fighting. Because with my broken leg any fighting would be one-way traffic.

179

I tried to think what I could do. I could take all the pillows away so he couldn't smother her, but that wasn't going to be enough if he brought his little gun.

I wished again that I'd made a go for the little gun when we were in the alley by the White Castle. I might of stopped all of this. Chuckie hadn't seen me for a long time. He didn't know about how much stronger I am now and not a skinny kid anymore. George got a taste of Kelly being strong and I'm even stronger than her.

But I didn't go for the gun, so here I was. If Chuckie showed up at the door about the only thing I could do was to scream my head off and make Alison come running and call for security.

Would that be enough?

I rolled out in the hallway to look for Alison again so I could explain about it all. Only the hallway was empty.

If I screamed my head off and tried to keep my wheelchair between Chuckie and the bed, what good would it be if nobody heard me? If Chuckie went ahead and killed Kelly's mom and nobody but me saw him, Steponkus and the judge wouldn't believe me telling he did it any more than they believed he killed George from what I told them already.

But then Alison came back into the hallway out of another room. She looked like she was going to turn a different way, but she saw me and came over. "Do you need something?"

"The woman in the coma, Mrs. Kovic . . ."

"Yeah?"

"She's in danger tonight."

"The doctors don't think there's any immediate risk, Mr. Prince. And honestly, patients in Mrs. Kovic's condition very rarely pass away without giving us some warning signs."

"I don't mean medical danger. It's the guy who hit her on the head and put her in the coma in the first place. He got released by the police today."

"Oh yes?"

"They say they don't have hard evidence on him but, truth is, when Freda wakes up she'll testify it was him that did it to her. And, for sure, he'll figure that out. So I think he's going to come here and try to kill her and it could even be tonight."

Alison looked at me hard, and I could tell she didn't know if she should take it seriously.

I said, "Look, why don't you call the police and ask them?"

"Are you on medication, Mr. Prince?"

"The one in charge of the case is Sergeant Steponkus. Call her and check it. Meanwhile I'm going to stay by the bed and talk, but you should be on the lookout for if I scream and shout, because that will mean Chuckie got in there somehow." And I left her in the hallway to think about it all.

But once I was back by the bedside and looking at Kelly's mom again, I didn't know what I could talk to her about.

I didn't feel like talking again to ask why she hated me so much. It all made me cry before, along with Little Joe's blocks. If it went into the part of her brain that was listening in the first place, fine. But I wasn't going to say it over and over, the same thing.

So I didn't know what to say. I could of gone back out into the hall and to ask Alison if she had a book I could borrow, or even the phone book. But instead of deciding, I just started to talk about everything that happened in the last week and a half, beginning with when Kelly left me to go live in the apartment. And I talked about how with Kelly gone I couldn't help but go down to Berringers, for just a drink, and that's where I met up with George, only it didn't turn out to be the accident that I thought it was at the time.

I was about to tell her how Kelly ran into Chuckie and George outside the Kroger when Alison came into the room and she had a man with her in a security uniform.

"Oh good," I said to them.

Only it wasn't so good, because the man looked annoyed. "Nurse Krantzler tells me you were talking about killing somebody, pal. You want to tell me what that's about?"

"It's not me killing anybody. It's the guy who did this . . ." And I pointed to Kelly's mom with the bandages on her head. "The cops let him go today because of not enough hard evidence. It was even on the TV news."

The security man looked at Alison. She shrugged.

I said, "It's Chuckie Gardner, the guy they released. He's going to work out Mrs. Kovic is a danger to him if she wakes up."

And I could see by how the security guy looked at Alison again that what I was saying was different from what Alison told him already. "So it's not this guy?" he asked her.

"He wasn't making a whole lot of sense, Win, and he talked about screaming and shouting," Alison said. "I figured it was better to call you now instead of wait for something to happen."

"Is that true?" the guy said to me, and on his uniform the nametag read, "Winston Wildpark." "Did you threaten to scream and shout?"

"Only if the guy that was released got here into the room," I said. "With my leg like this—which the same guy did to me, by the way, by shooting me—there's nothing else I would be able to do."

"Shooting?" Wildpark looked at Alison. She shrugged again. "Look, pal," he said to me, "the police haven't told us about any danger to any of our patients."

"Maybe they didn't work it out, because I only just worked it out myself a little while ago."

Wildpark sighed. "A man down already, and now this."

"Call Sergeant Steponkus at the IPD," I said.

"Yeah, I think I'll do that. And if they want special security on this patient, then they can damn well send somebody over, because I don't have the manpower." And he turned and walked out, taking Alison by the elbow and saying, "Keep an eye out just in case. I'll call IPD and let you know what they say."

And then I was back with Kelly's mom all by myself again.

I thought about where I was in the story, which was Chuckie and George in the parking lot at the Kroger and Kelly about to walk by and notice George's funny-colored Jetta. But then I stopped.

It was the first time I thought to wonder why they were in the parking lot of the Kroger in the old neighborhood. Why there?

George lived out in the middle of the reservoir, which was miles away. I didn't know where Chuckie really lived, but the Kroger in the old neighborhood was a funny place to meet and talk in George's car unless there was a reason. With guys like them it wouldn't be for old times' sake.

The only reason I could think of was because maybe it was convenient for Chuckie. So did that mean Chuckie's place—the one the cops couldn't find to search in for the gun and the money—Chuckie's place was somewhere near the Kroger? I bet it was.

"Wow," I said out loud to Kelly's mom. And right away what I wanted to do was tell Steponkus. There was a problem, though, and it was that I didn't have the number of the IPD with me. But Alison probably had a phone book and she had a phone as well. So I went out to ask her.

Alison was sitting behind the counter where the nurses sit when there's nothing much to do. She saw me when I came out and stood up. "Mr. Prince?"

"I need to call the police."

"Is something wrong?"

"I just figured something out that Sergeant Steponkus is going to want to know, but I don't have the number."

She looked at me hard. "You want to call the police?"

"Can I use your phone here? I'll pay you back."

I could see her think about it all. Then she took a deep breath and brought a phone up from behind the counter where I couldn't see it. Then she got a phone book. "Where would this sergeant be based? Downtown?"

"Yeah."

So she looked up the downtown number and dialed it and then gave me the receiver.

When it answered it said, "Hello. You have reached the Indianapolis Police Department Downtown District. If this is an emergency please hang up and dial nine-one-one. Our normal business hours are from eight a.m. to four p.m. Monday through Friday. If you would like to leave a message at the tone please state your name, telephone number and purpose for your call. This is the Indianapolis Police Department Downtown District. Have a great day." Then there was a tone.

I said, "This is Joe Prince and I need for Sergeant Steponkus to come and see me or call me or something as right away as possible because I've got a new idea about where Chuckie lives. But tonight I won't be in my own room. I'm going to stay downstairs on four by Kelly's mom's bed to protect her in case Chuckie shows up tonight, because he'll want her dead when he thinks of it. So that's where I'll be." I couldn't think of what else to say so I hung up.

I didn't know what more I could do. I gave the phone back to Alison and said, "Thanks."

"Think nothing of it."

I went back into Kelly's mom's room.

I sat there and watched her for a while before I started talking again. I didn't have my heart so much into telling her the whole story, but I also didn't have anything else to say. Truth is,

I was getting a little tired again, even if I did have a nap after dinner upstairs.

But I settled myself to the job and picked up the story again at where Kelly saw George's Jetta and when she stopped to look at its colors, she saw Chuckie and George inside, of all people. When I went on to say about how the Kroger parking lot was a funny place for the two of them to meet unless it was close to where Chuckie lived, it all sounded right to me.

So then I told Kelly's mom about how George tried to stick his tongue down Kelly's throat and how Kelly slugged him and knocked him over and how I bet George would never try that again with Kelly, even if he was still alive. And while I was telling it, I thought that Kelly's mom would be pretty proud of her little girl, hearing how she defended herself, and was strong.

I was proud of her too, and I had to stop talking then because I missed Kelly so bad. It was only after a while that I could start up telling the story again.

Next I told Freda the part about how Kelly saw a German shepherd dog in Chuckie's car. And I told her how for anybody except the judge today that would prove that Chuckie killed George, because the cops took a German shepherd dog off the houseboat that later already knew Chuckie even though the ID parade didn't go right.

And then I stopped because I thought of something else.

When the cops took the witness dog off the houseboat it didn't have a collar on. If that was the way Chuckie kept the dog at home, then probably the dog was left to run free when she needed a walk because there was no place for a leash. Running free, the dog was sure to know her way around the neighborhood, and also know the way home. So what if the police took the witness dog to the Kroger and walked her around or even let her go? If they did that, then maybe the witness dog would lead the cops to where Chuckie really lived.

I got all excited when I thought of that, and I wanted to talk to Steponkus now, only there was no point calling again since it wasn't eight a.m. yet, or even close.

So I just sat there, breathing hard, and wanting to do something, but also feeling tired and not wanting to leave Kelly's mom alone. What I did was take up and start telling the story some more.

It was when I got to the part about the *Sunbird* and the girlfriend and how I dreamed that the girlfriend came on a scooter to where my truck wasn't and turned into Kelly that a funny thing happened. It was another dream, only this time I knew it was a dream all along and instead of the girlfriend coming on the scooter it was Linda. And this time it was me getting onto the scooter behind her and Linda drove us away.

Where she drove us was to a quiet place by the shore, under tree branches that hung over us like a sheet. And Linda said, "Time for dessert."

And even though I knew it was a dream, I was hungry for the dessert and I knew it wasn't ice cream. She began to take my clothes off and I said, "Be careful with my leg."

"Which one?" she said, and she laughed, and it was a pretty laugh, kind of like bells in the way that tapping glasses with a pencil can be like bells.

And then she began to take her clothes off too, which wasn't her nurse uniform but was ordinary clothes. Only she had a bikini underneath like the *Sunbird* girlfriend did, only instead of becoming Kelly like the last dream this time it stayed Linda, and I could see why her body was so warm and comfortable when it was up close to me.

When she was in the bikini she stopped undressing. She asked me, "Do you want to do this, Joe? Do you?"

And I knew she was meaning did I want to do it because of Kelly.

But I did want to. I really did. "Yes," I said. "Yes." And she took a step toward me with her arms out, only then I woke up.

It was still dark through the window so it wasn't morning yet. I was shaking when I woke up from the Linda dream. Even though I knew in the dream that I was dreaming, I also knew that in the dream I really really wanted to do it with Linda. And that wasn't what I wanted to want at all.

It was only a dream, but it still upset me because I thought I was past all that. I thought my days away from Kelly and not doing anything bad meant I was grown up and more mature now. Only in the dream I wasn't all over it again.

I sat there alone by Freda's bed for a long time. My leg itched something awful under the cast and I didn't feel sleepy anymore at all. Especially in case if I did go back to sleep I would dream about Linda again and it would go even farther. Maybe it was silly for me to worry about a dream, but I did such a lot of hard work being alone from Kelly and not being bad that I hated to risk it.

After a while I began to wonder if the dream meant I was never going to be grown up and more mature. That got me sad, because it was so hard to be without Kelly even if I knew in my head that it was an important thing for me to learn how to do.

The real problem was that I didn't want to be apart from Kelly. What I wanted was to go home to Kelly and Little Joe. But that would mean leaving Kelly's mom alone with no one to protect her.

I watched Freda for a while and listened to her breathe. And even though I knew it would help fix Chuckie once and for all if she would wake up, right then I wouldn't of minded much if she just died and called it all quits.

16

Sometime I must of gone to sleep again because then it was morning and bright. There across the lap of my chair was a hospital table and it had a tray of food on it, cereal and fruit and coffee.

I shook myself to be wide awake, and what I knew first was that my mouth tasted awful and also that I needed to go to the bathroom. I moved the food-table away and rolled into the hallway even though there was a bathroom in Kelly's mom's room. Using that one didn't feel right.

At the nurses' desk I asked for a men's room. There was a new nurse with a label of *Geraldine* and she pointed to where the men's room would be in the corridor outside Freda's women's ward. And she said that Alison told her about me when the shifts changed because usually they don't allow visitors to stay overnight, especially not men. "I hope you liked your breakfast," Geraldine said, "because I said to myself, I'm gonna take care of any boy that looks after his mother-in-law so good. I'm a mother-in-law myself."

I found the bathroom, and even though there wasn't a toothbrush or anything, when I also rinsed my mouth out it felt better, too. It was only then that I remembered there was food waiting for me, and I was glad about it because now I was hungry.

I only stopped on my way back to Kelly's mom's room to ask Geraldine if there was any news about the police for me.

"The police? What's a nice boy like you want with them?" So Alison must not of said anything to her about how Kelly's mom was in danger from being killed by Chuckie. I began to think if I ought to tell Geraldine myself when she said, "But while you were gone doing your business there was a gal went in to see your momma-in-law."

"A gal? Was she a really big one?" I hoped it was Steponkus coming here like I asked.

"No, no, she's just a little gal. But you like 'em big, do you, Joe?" and Geraldine laughed, because she was big, only not tall, too, like Steponkus.

At least a little one would be Cayenne, and that was almost as good because she'd know how to tell Steponkus about Freda being in danger from Chuckie. Maybe Cayenne even came to tell me I could have the witness dog. That was better than ever now, because of the idea I had of how the dog could lead us to where Chuckie really lived. Maybe they'd find the gun there that he shot me with, and also the money he stole with George and killed him for.

Only when I got into Kelly's mom's room it wasn't Cayenne. It was Lee, the neighbor.

"Hi again," she said.

Geraldine was right—she was only little, and also pale, but this time she looked more dressed up. I wondered if maybe she was on her way to work, whatever it was.

"You're back," I said. And I thought about how for Lee to be here again Kelly's mom must of shown Lee more friendliness than she ever showed me, even though I was the father of her grandson.

"Is that your breakfast?" Lee asked about the tray of food. "Because I figured it probably wasn't Mrs. Kovic's, unless she woke up overnight."

"She didn't wake up." We both looked at the bed then and

189

Kelly's mom looked grayer to me today. But how do you tell, really, when someone's in a coma? Do they have good days and bad days? I didn't know. She was the first coma person I ever knew. "And, yeah, Geraldine, the nurse, she left some breakfast for me."

"Don't let me stop you eating it, Joe," Lee said.

"Well . . ."

"Go on. I can see you're hungry."

So I rolled up beside the bed and pulled the table back over my lap like I found it when I woke up. I started with the corn flakes and poured some milk from a jug over them.

"Is your coffee cold?" Lee asked.

I felt the cup. "Yeah." I shrugged. "Doesn't matter."

"They've got to have a microwave somewhere for the nurses. If I can find it, I can heat that up for you."

I thought for a minute. "It is better hot," I said.

Lee got up and took my coffee cup out into the hall. While she was gone I ate the cereal and then started on the fruit that was there in a bowl. When she came back I could see the coffee was steaming now out of the mug.

"There you are, sir," she said when she put it down. "Let me know when you'd like your free refill."

I laughed. "Thanks."

"No problem."

I ate more fruit and when I finished it I put some milk in the coffee.

"Do you want sugar?" Lee said. "I'm sure there'd be sugar in the nurse's kitchen."

"I don't need sugar, but thanks."

"Sweet enough as you are, huh?"

"I guess today I am. But you are being nice. I guess you must be a really nice person altogether, if you visit Freda without even knowing her that well."

"You're going to make me blush."

"Don't do anything you don't want to do."

"The nurse said how you'd been here all night long. You must really care about Mrs. Kovic."

I didn't want to tell her what I really thought about Freda and what Freda thought about me. "Well, I guess."

"If you spend every night in here with her, people will start talking."

"Then they can come and do it instead of me, because of how she's got a better chance to wake up if somebody talks to her."

"Is there any change in whether they think she'll get better?"

"Not that I know. There hasn't been a doctor since I got here last night."

And then, almost like it was magic of me to say it, a doctor came through the door and Geraldine was right behind him.

"Well, hello," the doctor said. "Having a party?"

"No," I said. "I'm here because—"

He held up a hand. "Just joking. You're Mr. Prince, aren't you?"

"Yeah." He was a shortish guy, but with a thick chest like he worked out. Maybe forty?

"Well, I'm Doctor Hallarson," he said. "And Geraldine tells me that you've been at the bedside with . . ." He looked at his chart. "With Mrs. Kovic all night long. Have you noticed any changes in her over that time?"

"What changes?"

"Any variation in the way she was breathing, for instance."

I thought about it. "No. She stayed the same a lot."

He went to the bedside and took Kelly's mom's arm to feel her pulse. Then he looked in her eyes with a little flashlight by holding up her eyelids. "Hmmm."

"How is she?" I couldn't help asking then. "Because it would be a really good thing if she could wake up."

"I'm sure it would." And for a while he did things like rub the skin on her arm and scratch the soles of her feet.

While he was writing stuff down I said, "I mean it would be good for her to wake up for more than just herself."

"Oh yes?"

"Because if she could wake up and remember who did it to her, then she could put away a bad murderer."

"I hate to be a pedant," Dr. Hallarson said, "but if she wakes up then the person who did this wouldn't have murdered her."

"He murdered somebody else," I said.

Dr. Hallarson turned to look in my face. "Really?"

"Maybe you saw it on the TV. It's the Houseboat Murder."

He thought and then nodded slowly. "I think maybe I did see something about that."

"And the same guy did this to me." I pointed to my leg. "He shot it."

"Well, we'd better hope that Mrs. Kovic wakes up, eh?" He wrote a couple of more things, then said, "And I think the signs are pretty good."

"Really?" I said.

"I detect some improvements in her retinal responses."

"You do?"

"And what that means is that I think Mrs. Kovic is a good candidate for a new protocol that's been developed for short-term coma patients."

"What does that mean?" I said.

"It means that I am going to take Mrs. Kovic to theater . . ." He looked at his watch. "I can probably squeeze her in late this afternoon. And with a small surgical procedure followed by a new combination of drugs I think there is chance—a very good chance, in fact—that tomorrow or the next day she will regain consciousness."

"Wow. That's great."

"A miracle of modern medicine," Dr. Hallarson said. "We should have her back in her room by . . ." And he looked at his watch again. "I'd say we'll have her back in the room by about nine tonight. After she's had a night's sleep, we'll find out tomorrow if it worked."

"Nine. Got it," I said. Kelly's mom was going to wake up, probably. Wow.

The doctor turned to Lee. "There are never any guarantees, of course, but if I were a betting man, my dollar would certainly go on your mother to wake up tomorrow." And then he left, with Geraldine following.

"That'd be a good trick," Lee said when they were gone. "My mother's been dead for fifteen years."

"He thought that you—"

"I know, I know."

And I could see on her face that she was kind of agitated now. "Are you all right?" I said.

She didn't say anything for a minute until it was, "I sure wish my father died back then instead of Mom."

I could see she was thinking a lot of things inside. "You miss her, huh?"

"I missed her every day till I grew up enough to get away from there," and she was crying now.

I was on the side of the bed where the box of tissues was, and I twisted around to get them for her. Because of the chair there wasn't much I could do except throw them close to her side of the bed and they bounced off Freda's leg and onto the floor.

But she said, "Thanks," and picked them up and blew her nose.

I wondered if maybe somehow missing her own mom was why she came in to see how Kelly's mom was doing.

She used some tissues, threw them away in a wastebasket and

stood up. "I think I better be running along now, Joe. Nice to see you again."

"You too."

And then she was gone out the door.

I wondered if maybe when Kelly's mom did wake up, Lee might tell her how I sat with her and tried to think of things to talk about. It sure would be nice if Freda didn't hate me so much when this was over. That way, the next time there was a funeral I could go too. It was good that I was more grown up and mature now, but if Kelly never left me alone again for days at a time, it wouldn't matter.

I was thinking about that while I finished my breakfast, and my coffee. And I was a little bit sad that Lee was gone because I would of liked it to be made hot again and maybe a free refill, too.

Then Geraldine came into the room. "Your little friend gone?"

"Yeah."

"Well, Mr. Prince, we've had a call from the eighth floor, and they would like you to return to your room so you'll be sure to be there when your own doctor's on her rounds."

"OK," I said, and truth is, I was happy to hear it. First because my doctor might tell me I could go home to Kelly and Little Joe, and also because I didn't sleep very well in the wheelchair. It sure would be nice to get out of it. I've heard of bedsores, but I wondered if you ever get wheelchair sores. Anyway, I went back up to eight.

And when I got there it was Linda on duty. "Welcome back, Joe," she said. "We missed you."

"I came back up for the doctor."

"She'll want you in your bed. Care for some help?"

I was going to say no, but instead I said, "Yes." And it was just as well, because all my body was pretty tired and even with

Linda's help my leg hurt.

"Did you get any breakfast down there, Joe?"

"Geraldine gave me some."

"Who?"

"The nurse on four."

"Well, if you didn't get enough of what you want, just let me know." And Linda went back to the hallway or to some other patients.

But I wasn't hungry. Now that I was back in my own bed what I was was tired. It wasn't long before I was asleep again, even with all the light and the noise that was around.

And then it was afternoon and Kelly was by my bed. "Kell? Is that you?"

"Who else would it be?"

"I mean, you're really you and not a dream?" But by then I already knew she was her, and she also brought in Little Joe. "Have you been here long?"

"About twenty minutes."

"You should of woken me up."

"You looked so calm. It was like seeing Little Joe asleep."

And I knew it was her love talking. And I sure loved her too. I loved them both. I said, "Can I hold him?"

"Sure." And she lifted him up for me.

It was wonderful to have the little fella in my arms again, and hold him and let him play with my fingers.

"He's glad to see his daddy," Kelly said.

And Little Joe was full of smiles for me and chuckles when I tickled him. I almost melted, I loved it so much to hold him like that.

"He can't be as glad as his daddy is to see him," I said.

And then I remembered about Dr. Hallarson. "Kell, when I was with your mom this morning the doctor came in."

"I know, Joe. I was down there before I came up here. They told me what they're going to try. I even had to sign some things, but I don't see how it can hurt anything to see if it works."

She seemed pretty calm and not at all excited. I said, "What Dr. Hallarson told me was that he'd bet his dollar on it working."

"Well, we'll see."

She was still only quiet about it, but probably she was just tired with worry about her mom, plus all the other things that were going on.

I said, "There's no guarantees, I know. But anyway I'll go down there again tonight after nine."

"They told me how you spent the whole night there with Momma last night, Joe. That's really sweet of you."

"I want to help her wake up."

"But we need you to get better, too."

"I'll get better." And just about then Little Joe went to sleep in my arms, and also I remembered another thing to talk to Kelly about. "Kell?"

"What?"

"I did something with Cayenne I hope you don't mind."

"Joseph?"

"No, no, nothing like that. What I did was ask Cayenne to ask Steponkus if we could have the dog."

"What dog?"

"The witness dog. The one that the ID parade didn't work out right with."

"Oh. Chuckie's dog."

"You know they let Chuckie go, right?"

"I know."

"So I thought, since the witness dog hates Chuckie so much and barked as soon as she saw him, I thought it would be a

196

good thing to have the dog with us, in case Chuckie ever comes around—not that I think he will. In fact I'm sure he won't, but it still seems like a good idea." I didn't want to scare her, but I also wanted her to have the protection.

Kelly thought about it for a minute and then she said, "I'm happy to have the dog, Joe. I like dogs."

"Oh good. Great. I'm glad you didn't mind. Because I thought when I'm back working in my truck the dog might be good to leave with you and Little Joe if they still haven't locked Chuckie away by then."

She was quiet then. I figured it was just from her being tired overall instead of being afraid about Chuckie.

Well, maybe Kelly would feel even better once I got to talk to Steponkus about how the witness dog could help catch Chuckie by finding where he really lived from starting at the Kroger. But for the time being we were all quiet for a while, all three of us, including Little Joe asleep.

Only then Linda came in and said, "Mr. Prince, I hate to interrupt you and your lady friend, but we need to give you lunch so you'll be done when it's time for doctor. Shall I bring it in now?"

Kelly said, "I ought to go anyway. I have to go to Momma's apartment and meet an assessor from the insurance company about getting the fire damage fixed."

And even though I'd rather of spent more time with Kelly and Little Joe in my arms, I said, "OK." Whatever Kelly needed to do I wanted to help with, even if it was only not to get in the way of it. "It'll be good if the apartment can be fixed up again ready for her to move back into it when she wakes up and feels better."

"Joe?"

Kelly was looking at me in the eyes now. "What?"

"I've got something to ask you, too."

"What?"

"If Momma gets better, I want to be with her until she's strong enough to live alone again."

I didn't understand. "You want to move away again and live with her? But I thought we were OK, Kell."

"I didn't mean that, Joe. I want Momma to live with us."

"With us?"

"Until she's strong again."

"Oh."

"Is that OK? I could move back to her place, if you'd rather, but . . ."

I sure didn't want Kelly back at her mom's place again if I could help it. "It's OK, Kell," I said. "Anything's OK if we're together in it."

"Thank you, Joe." And as she took Little Joe from my arms, she gave me a kiss on my lips. It was only a light kiss, but it was about the sweetest kiss there could be.

As soon as Kelly pushed Little Joe out in his own kind of wheelchair, Linda was there again to set up the food table over my lap, only I wasn't that hungry now.

Kelly's mom living with us? Where would she sleep? Even if I cleared out the utility closet in the kitchen, I'd bet my dollar that Kelly wouldn't let us put her mom in it even if a bed fit. She'd put her mom in our bedroom, even though it would mean moving Little Joe's crib out of there along with us. The only other possible place was setting Freda up somehow in the living room.

And how was Kelly going to feel about me and her being together, even when Freda and Little Joe were both asleep? Would it have to be out in the truck again, like it was sometimes before I had my own house?

"Joe?"

Another thing I didn't know was if her mom could have a relapse of not being able to talk, once she talked enough to ID Chuckie and put him back in jail. Because the other last thing I wanted around my house was Kelly's mom's screechy voice going all the time. It was about louder than Little Joe's loudest crying.

"Joe?"

Or maybe Lee would come and visit and take Kelly's mom out for walks in a wheelchair. Long walks . . .

"Joe? Are you all right?"

"What? Oh." And it was Linda with my lunch, which was a tuna-fish sandwich and a salad and some fruit and a cookie. And coffee.

17

I only woke up again after lunch when the doctor was there and Linda shook my shoulder.

"Sorry to interrupt your beauty sleep, Mr. Prince," Dr. Jepson said. "I can see you need it. But I've managed to get you a slot with a physiotherapist today."

"What?" My head felt dusty on the inside, like there was a sandstorm in there that made it hard to see what I was hearing.

"Phys-i-o-ther-a-py. You've got an appointment in . . ." Dr. Jepson looked at her watch. "Thirty-five minutes. I just came by to make sure you haven't had any major setbacks overnight. How do you feel?"

"Feel?"

"Fe-el . . . Any pain in your leg, for instance?"

"Only when it hurts." Then I worked out that was a kinda stupid thing to say. I laughed.

"If you're joking about it, there can't be too much wrong. Well, let's see what we can see. Are you decent?" And she pulled the sheet aside off my leg like it was a magician and a tablecloth. "Oh my."

Then the doctor poked around my leg and pushed on my feet and tapped the cast. Some of it hurt, but I didn't say anything in case it slowed down about my going home. Only she said, "Tell me if it hurts."

"I guess some of it, maybe a little."

"You'd be in trouble if it didn't, Mr. Prince."

"OK, it hurts, especially when you push and twist."

She stood back. "And you're eating all right? And taking your pills?"

"Sure."

"Although I gather you didn't spend last night in your own bed. Naughty boy." She flicked the cast with her finger.

It only hurt a little. "I was in the wheelchair."

"When I said it was good to spend time in the chair, I didn't mean all the time. Bed rest is important too."

"That's what I was doing now."

"Well, what I'm going to do now is order a couple of blood tests so we can see where we are with your insides." She wrote on her clipboard. "And I'm also going to have your leg X-rayed. If none of that shows any problems, we can think about letting you go home."

"Home? Really?"

"As long as you're careful. Where you live, are there a lot of stairs?"

"No stairs, except two up to the front porch."

"And is there someone who can look after you?"

"There sure is." I was getting excited. Going home!

"Well, I'll see you tomorrow, Mr. Prince." She turned to Linda. "Nurse, you may restore Mr. Prince's modesty now."

Going home . . . With Kelly . . . It was my dreams coming true. Maybe it would mean I wouldn't be the one talking when Kelly's mom woke up, but I could look after Little Joe when Kelly went to the hospital to visit. I could hardly believe it.

"Well, well, Joe," Linda said as she pulled the sheet back over my leg. "Happy to see me?"

Half an hour later I was in the physiotherapy place that was on the second floor. Jan, the physiotherapist, picked out the best size and kind of crutches for me. I never knew there could be so much to choose.

And then she had me use them, which really hurt and in more places than just my leg. "You'll get used to them, Mr. Prince," she told me, even though it felt like I never would.

It wasn't that I didn't want the crutches to work. It was just hard. It reminded me of jumping into the water when I was on the *Tia Maria*. I wanted it to be comfortable, natural, but whenever I did it all I really wanted was to get back onto the dry land of the houseboat again. Here, the crutches made the wheelchair look real good. Only for the *Tia* I did get ashore through the water in the end. So I would do this, too.

With practice I got better walking to the wall and back and the other things Jan said to do. And I also practiced getting in and out of the wheelchair with them, she showed me how there was a place already in the chair to fit the crutches like a holster so it would be easy to carry them around while I was wheeling.

Finally she said, "That'll do for today, Mr. Prince. Of course our real work will begin once we have that cast off your leg."

"This wasn't real?"

And there was something lopsided about her smile that made me scared for a minute. How long would I have to keep therapying? And was I really always going to have a limp?

But at least now I had my crutches. So all I had left was my blood tests and my X-ray before maybe Dr. Jepson would let me out to go home. I was soo happy about that. I hoped Kelly would be too.

But by the time I got back to my own room I didn't feel much like practicing with my crutches some more, even though Jan said it was always a good thing and also Linda said, "Hey, big boy, you going to show me how you can get yourself up?"

"I feel more like going to bed," I said.

And I did, and I pretended I didn't even hear when she said, "Works for me."

I never took so many naps in my life. Still, I was never shot before. Maybe they go together.

But my nap wasn't a long one because they took blood and then I had to go for the X-ray. By then it was the end of the afternoon which was when Cayenne came to visit me.

"Did something happen?" I said. "Did they arrest Chuckie?"

"No good news like that, Joe." She pulled up a chair by the bed and looked tired. "But who knows? Maybe soon."

"I have good news. The doctor says if I pass my blood tests and X-ray then I can go home, maybe tomorrow."

"Congratulations."

"Thank you."

"I know Kelly will be glad too. I talked to her a bit this morning."

"You did?"

"Kelly's involved in what happens with her mother, as well as things that relate to you being here, Joe."

"Did you hear the good news about Freda?" I said. "How the doctor down there, Dr. Hallarson, said he has a protocol she would be a good one to try it on. He even bet his dollar that she'll wake up after it. Probably tomorrow."

"It would certainly benefit everyone if Mrs. Kovic were to wake up."

"When she names Chuckie as the one who put her in the coma, Steponkus would have to put him in jail again."

"I know for a fact that Steph would love to do exactly that, Joe."

"Well I wish she'd believe me enough to lock Chuckie up again."

Cayenne looked like there was something she wanted to say to that, but she sighed instead. "They tell me you spent last night at Mrs. Kovic's bedside."

"Harry, the nurse there, told me it was good for somebody to talk to her."

"Are you planning to spend tonight with her, too? Because I want to make sure you know, Joe, that you don't have to go down there. I'm sure Mrs. Kovic will be fine, perfectly safe, even if you're not there."

And I was surprised that she said about being safe, because I only worked out Kelly's mom's danger yesterday. But Cayenne was smart, so I shouldn't be surprised if she worked it out too. "Truth is," I said, "I did stay there last night because Chuckie might sneak in to make sure she doesn't wake up."

"What would you do to protect Mrs. Kovic if Charles Gardner were to come into the room, Joe?"

"I'd shout. Or now I could hit him with one of my crutches. Did you see them?" I pointed to where they were in the chair.

"Well, the hospital does have security people. I'll make sure they know about the danger."

"Good. Thank you," I said. Though there was still the reason of talking to her, which couldn't hurt, as well as maybe not being around while Linda was on duty if she worked late. But I liked that Cayenne would tell other people about Chuckie's danger to Freda so that it wasn't all on me. "This way I can see how I feel when it comes to nine."

"Good."

Then I thought about the other thing I wanted to know from Cayenne. "Did you talk to Steponkus about me having the dog?"

"Ah." She pulled out her notebook. "Steph says that she is happy to release the dog into your custody once you're back home."

"Custody? Won't the dog really be ours?"

"It's a technicality. Steph only has the say-so about where the dog's kept if she's still a potential 'witness' in the case. Once the case is closed, the dog would go to the pound. So Steph says you should take her now and once the case is closed, she figures nobody at IPD will care or remember."

"OK. Custody sounds good that way," I said. "I asked Kelly and she's happy for the dog to live at our house too."

"Sounds like we have a deal," Cayenne said.

"Great." And it was, because the plan included me being at home again soon, even if maybe Kelly's mom would be there too, after she woke up.

And then Cayenne left because she had to go. I didn't get the chance to say how tired she looked and I only remembered later about how the witness dog could maybe be a witness again to find where Chuckie really lived.

I watched some TV then, and also all through dinner. Nowhere on the news was there anything about the Houseboat Murder or Chuckie. Or me.

Then I decided maybe I really ought to practice on my crutches some more, because Jan the physiotherapist told me the more I practiced the more comfortable they would be. So I got the crutches out from the chair holster and I was really careful about getting myself up to walk. I did it slow like Jan told me and she was right, because from the first few steps of walking it didn't hurt as much as I remembered.

I walked out into the hall, thinking I could show off walking to Linda. Only it was a guy at the nurse's desk. "Oh, hi," I said. "I thought you were going to be Linda."

He held up his hand in front of his face, like a mirror, and said, "Let me check. Nope. Not Linda. Just me, Paul. Can I do something for you?"

"No. That's OK." Then I said, "I'm the guy in Room C."

He looked on the board behind his chair. "That would make you Mr. Prince."

"Yup. I'm practicing my crutches."

"They're crutches, all right," Paul said, and then he went back to what he was already doing.

I turned to walk down the hall with the idea I would go to the ward door and back. Truth is, I was disappointed Linda wasn't there because she'd know how much progress it was for me to be on crutches now. Only then when I looked up to the end of the hall, it was Linda, who came out of a room on the side. I was going to call but she already saw me and came my way.

"I can walk," I said, and I did it in her direction, but I must of done it too fast because it began to hurt.

"Well, look at you, Joe," Linda said. "All erect."

"My plan was to walk to the ward door and back."

"I'm just on my way home, so I'll walk to the door with you."

"OK." Though my hurting leg reminded me to take it slow, and I did and didn't hurry and Jan was right. Walking now again didn't hurt as much as it did downstairs in Physiotherapy.

We were nearly at the end of the hall when Linda put a hand on my arm. "Will you be able to manage doors for yourself when you're on the crutches, Joe?"

"Doors?"

"You'll want to open and close doors when you go home, won't you? Going to the bathroom, or keeping your kid from following you around?" She pointed to a door that was marked for nurses.

Little Joe was too young to follow me, but I hadn't thought about doors. So I went to this one and balanced myself and opened the handle.

"Good," Linda said. "Now go in and see if you can close it behind you."

So I went in and she came in with me. It was a room with only a couple of chairs and a little table and a few kitchen things like a microwave.

"And close the door?"

So I closed the door, which I did with the handle instead of just pushing it to slam, which would of been the easy way, but kind of cheating. Like, if it was at night and I was going to the bathroom and Kelly was asleep I wouldn't want the door to slam.

"Good work, Joe," Linda said. "Good work."

"Thanks."

I was going to open the door again, but Linda slipped into the space between it and me. It wasn't a very big space.

"What are you doing?" I said.

"I like you, Joe."

And I could see the look in her eyes, and then I remembered how here we were in a little room, alone with the door shut.

She put her hand on my chest and it was hard for me to do anything about it because of keeping my balance on the crutches without hurting. It was even hard for me to back up away from her, but I tried. Then she put her other hand around my waist.

She said, "I know you're not up to much right now, and I know you think you owe something to blondie and her kid. But I want you to remember that when you're feeling better I'll be here. No big deal. Just a bit of fun. Whenever you're ready, just call the ward and leave me a message."

"No," I said. And I tried again to back up, even though it was against her grip.

"Don't play hard to get, Joe. I've seen the way you look at me when I'm around. And I know you like it when I'm close to you. Like now." And she gave me a little push closer, but then let me go.

And before I could say "No," again, she eased away from me to the side. "And I know I'll be hearing from you," she said, and then slid herself out of the door.

So I was standing there, in the nurses' room, and I was

breathing so hard and the blood was pumping around so much that I found one of the chairs and dropped myself on it. But I did it too fast and it hurt my leg like hell, which was a reminder again.

I was breathing but I was thinking too. I didn't look at Linda that way when she was around. Did I?

I didn't think I did.

But it was true that I liked it when she was close to me. Was that really bad for me to do? Or just natural, like the looking but not touching of some other woman would be?

But there was a problem with me. One that was somewhere deep inside me and about women who weren't Kelly. Even though it did not mean that I would ever call Linda to leave a message.

It was so hard to be more grown up. It seemed never to stop being a problem, especially catching me by surprise. That must be what being a grown up was—not doing just any old thing that happened to come up into your mind and you might feel like doing.

Because, as I sat there, I was glad that all Linda did to me today was put her hands on my chest and waist and talk. Truth is, if she'd of done some other things I might not of been strong enough to stop her from it.

I kept sitting there, and it was scary.

After a while, though, Paul, the new nurse, opened the door. When he saw me he said, "Oh. Fuck."

"Sorry," I said. "I'm just resting."

"Overdid it, huh?"

And I let him help me back to my room. And then I stayed in bed, resting, even though I didn't feel sleepy and I didn't even turn the TV on.

18

About twenty past nine I went down to four where Kelly's mom was. And Geraldine was still the nurse, which was a surprise to me. "I'd of thought you'd be back home by now to get some rest at the end of your shift," I told her.

"No rest for the wicked and, honey, when I get going, there's nobody more wicked than me." And it was a joke and she laughed and it was nice how she was cheery. Then she said, "I took me a nap this afternoon. How about you?"

"I got some sleep, and some crutches too."

"And a fine pair of crutches they are," she said, because she could see them holstered in the chair. "How you getting along with them?"

"They already hurt less the second time I tried."

"In a few days you'll forget you ever walked without them, believe me." She picked up a clipboard. "Before I forget, your mother-in-law's room has changed a little since this morning." She came out from behind her counter.

"Is that because she had the protocol?"

"It sure is." She tapped a finger on my forehead. "Nothing gets past that, does it? Well, you'll see that Mrs. Kovic has a few more bandages on her head now, and the doctor's had us turn the lighting down in the room. But don't you worry if you want to read. Just turn on the side light, or the TV if you want. It's not a problem."

"So I guess she didn't wake up yet."

"No, but you'll probably be aware of some changes in her. For instance, she shifts position in bed by herself sometimes, and she wasn't doing that before, was she?"

"She didn't move at all, except when one of you nurses came in to turn her so she didn't get sores." If Freda was moving herself in bed, that had to be good. It was about then that I began to believe that maybe one day Kelly's mom would wake up and solve everything.

So I went into Kelly's mom's room. And I saw the light Geraldine meant that I could turn on if I wanted. She came in with me and said, "Later on, if you come looking for me and you don't see me, I'll probably be in the nurses' kitchen."

"OK."

"Or maybe I'll just hop into one of the other beds in the ward for a few zees," she said laughing. "For some reason we're empty down here tonight. But either way if you need me and don't see me, just give me a shout, OK?"

"OK," I said.

"And remember, Joe, no need to get worried—or excited—if Mrs. Kovic turns herself over. But if she sits up and starts singing 'The Star Spangled Banner' now, that's something else altogether." And she left laughing, and I was alone with Kelly's mom.

Even though the light was pretty dark, I could see the new bandages on Freda's head, about two-thirds now. It made me wonder what it was the doctor did to her. Still, it had to be something to her head, because of that's where her coma was.

So I rolled my chair up close to the table where the light was, too, and the TV remote control. I thought then about if I should try to talk to Kelly's mom, but I remembered how long it was last night when I tried to talk all the time. I ran out of things to say and now tonight there wasn't much new that I could think of to add. I could tell her about the crutches, but that wouldn't last a whole night. And I felt more like watching the TV anyway, so I did that.

I found a comedy on and then another one. I wondered if Kelly's mom watched these on her TV at home. If she did then the voices would be familiar to her. Truth is, TV that she ever watched regularly would be a whole lot more familiar to her than my voice was. Thinking that way, I didn't feel I was letting her down so much by having the TV do all the talking for a while.

Then later I found I was thinking about Linda and about how she thought that I had been looking at her that way, when truth is, she was the one looking at me.

So I turned off the TV I wasn't watching and I started talking. "I don't know how it was when you were young," I said to Kelly's mom, "but these days anybody can get into a lot of trouble just by looking. Like, there's this nurse upstairs in my own ward, and she looks at me, that way, and . . ." And then I stopped because I wondered if Kelly's mom would know what I was talking about.

"Do you know what I mean, Freda? Because maybe in your young days people didn't look at each other like they do now. These days all you have to do is see somebody look at you and you could be halfway to getting into trouble with them. I used to do that, but now that I'm with Kelly so maturely, I'm different, even if I did slip when Kelly was away with you for the funeral."

Then Kelly's mom moved some. And as I listened to her, I could tell that her breathing was different from the way it was last night. Altogether it felt more like she could be listening to me tonight, which was amazing and wonderful if it was true and from whatever Dr. Hallarson did to her.

But then it made me think maybe I ought to be careful of what I might be saying. If part of her brain was hearing me, then part of it might remember too. So maybe it would be good not to remind her too much about the things that made her hate me in the first place. Maybe she could even wake up liking me better for Kelly, especially now we had Little Joe.

I said, "You always hear about how parents are more restrictive of their own children than they acted when they were young themselves. That can be cause the parents don't want their kids to make the same mistakes, but it can also be cause the parents don't have any idea what mistakes the kids will make anyway. My dad went to Berringers in his young days, and so did my mom, sometimes, although not later when she had her drunk problem. And truth is, I met Kelly myself at Berringers when she was there with her friend Nadine. I don't know if you knew Nadine. Kelly never said if she brought Nadine home any more than she ever brought me. Nadine was wild, and the idea I had from Kelly was you disapproved of the side of Kelly herself that was wild too. But that's what I'm saying. Did you know what used to happen out there when we were kids? Were you like that too, or were you as much different from us when you were young as you are now?"

And then I stopped talking. Saying all that made me realize I didn't know any more about Freda's own life than she did about mine. We never sat and talked before she hated me and Kelly had to pretend she wasn't dating me. I remember once when Kelly and I were downtown and we walked around a corner and there was Kelly's mom coming the other way. The poison in her eyes was like a dagger I can remember even now.

But then I thought, maybe once the protocol worked and Kelly's mom was awake and Chuckie was in jail where he belonged, maybe that would be a good time for me and Freda to try to start over. Especially if she was already going to be in the same house with us, recovering.

What was funny was how I was with her all night last night

and during that time I talked to her more than all of the rest of my life put together. If she woke up and remembered it then she'd know all about Chuckie and the Houseboat Murder. Or maybe she'd only remember bits and not know how they went together. Like the dog and a girl in a bikini and a shotgun. It would be like a puzzle.

Maybe tonight it would be a good idea for me to tell it all to her again. Maybe she could fill in the bits she didn't get the first time and she'd wake up knowing everything that happened after she didn't take me to the funeral.

Yeah, it was a good idea for me to tell it all to her again, and that solved what I should talk about tonight. But, truth is, I was also tired again. So I decided to save it to start later on in the night. What I did now was close my eyes a few minutes first.

And then there was a woman silhouetted in the doorway to Kelly's mom's room. All her face and her front was dark with only her outline for me to see. That was enough to see her shape wasn't a big one, like Geraldine or Steponkus. It was a little shape. Too little for Linda, or even Kelly or the *Sunbird* girlfriend. And I could also see it was too skinny for Cayenne. So who was it?

"Hello?" I said to the woman in the door. "Who's that?"

The silhouette woman didn't say anything back. What she did instead was come into the room my way, and she closed most of the door behind her so it was even darker than before except for the light from the hall that came through a glass panel above the door.

"Hello?" I said again. "Who's that? Who are you?" And I still didn't know. I didn't know if I was dreaming.

From not much more than shadows I could see the silhouette woman move to the end of the bed, and then she came around it to the same side as my wheelchair. I was about to get upset with her not answering who she was, but then she said, "I see you're here again tonight, Joe."

And because of her voice now I knew who it was. "Lee?"

She leaned against the bed then.

I said, "Are you real? Or am I dreaming?"

"I've never had anybody call me a dream before. You want me to pinch you? Is that what you're into, Joe?"

I figured now it wasn't a dream. But I was still way surprised that Lee would come to see Kelly's mom again, and so late.

I was going to ask what time it was but she said, "How's Freda? Did they do their operation?"

"The protocol? Yeah, they did it."

"And did it work?"

"She turns over by herself and she never did that before. And her breathing is different."

"But she didn't wake up?"

"Not yet."

"So why are you here?"

"Because I figured even if she didn't wake up yet, it must still be good for her to have somebody talk to her and at least it can't do any harm."

"What a devoted family man you are, Joe."

"So how come you're here now, Lee? Is it some job you have that ends late, and you stopped on your way home?"

"Something like that."

If it was only now that Lee was on her way home from work, it was a long day for her—like the one Geraldine had. "So are you a nurse or something?"

But she gave a laugh at that, so I guess she wasn't. She said, "If you intend to stay here, Joe, would you like me to get you a drink? A can or something? Or a coffee from the kitchen?"

Truth is that sounded good because of how water can be boring to drink all night. I said, "A pop that isn't diet, thanks.

You could ask Geraldine, but I'm sure she'll say OK for you to get it, because she's real friendly."

"Who's Geraldine?"

"The nurse on duty."

"No one's at the desk out there."

"Maybe she's in the kitchen herself."

"Nobody was there when I came in."

"No?"

"The door was open."

"Well, she could be having a nap in one of the empty rooms She said she might do that because of how she worked so long a day. She's the same nurse who was on when you came in here this morning."

"Oh yeah?" I saw now that Lee was moving toward the door. "I'll look for that pop." And she went out.

It left me to think about Lee being there, and how I was surprised at it. Because it wasn't the usual thing I'd expect for a neighbor to do, especially not twice in one day when she didn't know Kelly's mom all that well in the first place.

And then I wondered if maybe there might be more to how Lee knew Freda than she told me so far. Maybe she owed Freda money, though I never heard of Kelly's mom lending anybody a nickel. But she sure had enough to take Kelly and Little Joe with her to the funeral in Las Vegas, and that was even before she got any inheritance that she might set Kelly up in business with.

And then I wondered if it was possible for Lee and Freda to know each other better than Lee ever said in a different way. Could they be friends like *that?* Even though Freda was old and witchy and Lee was young, though not exactly pretty? I didn't really believe that's how they knew each other, but it made me smile to think of it.

But that made me think of another reason Lee might of come

to the hospital again, especially at night. Especially when she knew I might probably be here in Kelly's mom's room too. Maybe she didn't come in to see Freda at all.

I hadn't seen that look in Lee's eyes back when the light was good. But you don't always see it.

Or could she of thought she saw something in my eyes, only it wasn't there, like Linda?

I tried to remember if Lee ever said anything to me that might of meant something that way. All I could think of was how she said I could have a free refill.

And she was getting me a pop now . . .

But that didn't have to mean that. Did it?

It didn't even make sense to come in to the hospital for that. Not when she could already see I'm in a wheelchair with my leg in a big cast from being shot.

Yet she did come in at night, when it was already late.

Something was wrong with Lee coming to visit Freda again. Even if I couldn't work out for sure what it was.

And I did have plenty of time to think about it. Lee was away a long time. Maybe there were no pops left in the nurses' kitchen and she had to go look someplace else in the hospital.

And then, after all the thinking, I began to feel sleepy again. So maybe Lee was another dream after all.

But then Lee was back, and standing inside the door. I could see from the light behind her she had a can in her hand. She said, "Sorry it took so long, Joe."

"That's OK. I'm not going anywhere."

"You know, we could change that."

I didn't understand. "What?"

She came over and sat down on the bed—right in front of me. "Because I like you, Joe. I really do."

"What?"

"And I was thinking, maybe you and me, we could take your drink someplace else. Into another room, maybe. Or, even better, we could go outside for a while. It's a nice night out there. How long's it been since you had some fresh air? If I push your chair we could go about anywhere. Would you like that? You and me outside? We could have a little fun. I bet I could make you forget that broken leg if we were alone someplace. What do you say, Joe?"

So it was that after all. "Thanks, but—"

Lee slipped off the bed and went behind my wheelchair.

I said, "What are you doing?"

"Let's find a little privacy." She turned my chair around toward the door.

"Don't," I said.

"You maybe think you don't want to, but I bet you'd like it. Hey, we can take it slow, if that's what you want. Talk, see if anything pops up . . ." She laughed a laugh. "Because you're really hot, Joe. And I hear you've always had an eye for the ladies." She pushed me again. "And something else for them too."

But I didn't feel even a little temptation. I just put on my brake and grabbed my wheels.

"No," I said. "I don't want to."

"It'll be good. I promise. And we don't have to be away long."

"No."

She stopped trying to push then.

"I'm really sorry to say no to it," I said, "especially with you being a friend of Freda's. But Kelly's the only one I want now, no matter how I used to be before."

I couldn't see Lee, but I heard her give a big sigh. "Well, I tried."

"We can still talk here," I said. "In fact that would probably be a good thing for Freda."

"Fuck Freda." Lee went to the door and out of it.

And that caught me by surprise too, the same as Lee showing up in the first place did. Behind me I heard Kelly's mom turn over again. Maybe she was surprised about it all too.

I unlocked my chair and turned it around to face her. If she could hear stuff in her brain, then she must of heard me say no to Lee. "You heard that, right?" I said to her. "You heard how she wanted us to do it, but I said no, and all because I love Kelly so much."

I moved the chair back to where I had it by her bed in the first place. If Kelly's mom was hearing things in her brain better after the protocol, maybe now was a good time for me to start on telling her the whole story again. "It all began," I said, "when you took Kelly and Little Joe to the funeral, but left me behind."

But that's as far as I got because then the room door opened again. I thought maybe Lee brought back the pop she didn't leave behind when she left in a huff. Or maybe it was Geraldine after she came back from wherever she went.

But it wasn't either of them. This time the silhouette was a man. He took a look around from the doorway, and then he came in. Behind him was another silhouette who was Lee back again. She closed the door and we were in the dark.

"What's going on?" I said, but also I was feeling around for the little lamp that was on the table for me to read with.

"You should have gone with her, Joe," the man said, and the voice was Chuckie's.

19

Even though I was in Kelly's mom's room because I thought Chuckie might come, I never fully planned out what to do if he did.

A flashlight came on in my eyes. "How you doing, Joe?"

"What are you doing here?" I asked, even though why else would he come but to kill Kelly's mom.

"Just stopped by to see how things are going."

Then Lee said, "For Christ's sake, Chuck, get on with it."

"Shut up," Chuckie said to Lee, and he flashed the light at her like it was a whip.

"We're alone now," she said, "but who knows how long before the nurse comes back?"

"You worried about the nurse? Go stand at the door and look out for her then," Chuckie said.

And while they were talking I worked it out that if Chuckie had his little gun with him then there was nothing I could do to stop him. So I did the only thing I could do while I still could. "Help!" I shouted out. "He's going to kill Kelly's mom! Help! Help!" Maybe there was nobody outside the door like Lee said, but maybe at that very minute Geraldine was on her way back from wherever she went and would hear me.

But nothing happened from the hall. All that happened was Freda turned in her bed. What a time this would be for her to wake up . . .

Chuckie flashed the light back into my eyes. I could hardly

see from it, but I did see some movement of Lee going behind my wheelchair. And then I felt a real sharp point stabbing right in my neck.

"Ow!" I tried to push it away.

"Put your hands down," Chuckie said.

I heard the meanness in his voice, so I did it. "They're down, they're down," and then the stab wasn't quite so sharp in my neck anymore.

"Do you know what that is, Joe?" Chuckie said. "It's a plastic knitting needle, sharpened up. Do you like it? The metal detectors make it tough to get a gun in to a hospital anymore, but a knitting needle in a woman's handbag? Who cares about that?"

And Lee said in my ear, "Keep quiet, Joe, or you're a dead man."

I didn't know what to say to that.

Chuckie said, "She'll stick you like a pig. She grew up on a farm. She knows how."

And Lee pushed the point in harder again.

"C'mon, stop," I said, but I whispered it, so she eased up.

"Em's just making a point." Chuckie's laugh then was a nasty one. "But at least we know you won't be running away. So you're stuck in here, Joseph. Stuck? Get it?"

"Who are you?" I asked Lee. "Why does he call you Em?"

"Because my name is Emily," she said. "Emi-ly."

And then I understood it all. Lee wasn't Kelly's mom's neighbor at all. She was Emily Tuck, the alibi woman for Chuckie. Emi-lee. So when she came in to see Freda, it was only to see if Freda was awake and talking yet, so she could tell it back to Chuckie. I felt so stupid that it was only now I understood. Of course a witch like Kelly's mom wouldn't have a neighbor who cared enough to visit her in the hospital all those times.

Chuckie said, "Em even gave you a chance to get out of this,

Joe, if only you'd been smart enough to take it. But it's probably cleaner this way. I don't know why I didn't finish you off when I had the chance before. Old times' sake, I guess."

"It's still old times now," I said.

"Last time I thought you were going to run away from it all. Instead, you went to the cops."

"I couldn't run away anywhere with a shot leg, could I?"

"Well . . ." He gave a laugh.

"And I didn't go to the cops. They came to me, and found me when I was bleeding to death in front of the White Castle."

"You still didn't have to tell them anything."

"But it didn't matter, did it?" I said. "Sure, I told them you said you killed George because he was a twisted fuck and tried to screw you out of money. But they still let you go, didn't they? Whatever I said to them wasn't enough, and it's why you're here now and not in jail."

"Maybe it's why I'm not in jail," Chuckie said, "but the reason I'm here has nothing to do with you, Joseph." In the shadows I saw him pick up a pillow. "Nothing at all."

"But Kelly's mom's in a coma and can't even talk. She's been like that for days."

"But she might wake up. And it might be tomorrow."

"Even if she did," I said, "probably she wouldn't even remember it was you that hit her on the head in the first place. Remember Max in Union Station?"

Back when we were all kids in a gang Max knocked himself out from walking into an I-beam without looking and he didn't remember anything about the beam or what we did before it. Max was funny in his head for days.

But Chuckie said, "Screw Max. What matters is that this old woman might remember. Come on, Joe, if it was you in my shoes, would you want to take that chance?"

If it was me in his shoes, I'd take them off as fast as I could, but I didn't say that. I said, "Even if Freda does wake up and say stuff to the cops, why would they take that as evidence any more than what I told them already? They'd still let you go."

"Nice try, Joe. You've always been a trier."

But I could hear in his voice that me trying wasn't going to be enough for him to leave Kelly's mom alive in her coma.

Emi-lee said, "Get on with it, Chuck."

"You right. You right." Chuckie turned the light to Kelly's mom's bandaged head. "Poor old woman, in a coma and never going to coma out of it."

"Her bandages were in a different place before," Emi-lee said. Her voice said she didn't like it.

"They did some operation thing on her, didn't they?"

"Yeah, I guess."

"Well?"

Even while they were talking about Kelly's mom, I knew she wasn't the only one they were going to kill. So I said, "Don't forget to plan ahead with your story, Chuckie."

"What's that supposed to mean?"

"If I'm dead here, too, they'll know somebody did it to Freda and she didn't just die in her sleep."

The light came into my face again. "But we're not leaving you here, Joseph."

"You're not?"

"You're coming with us."

"I am?"

"What could be more natural in a hospital than two people pushing a guy out in wheelchair? Not that you'll be in any condition to enjoy the ride."

"Why not?" I said. "I like rides."

"I tried to get you out of here," Emi-lee said. "But you were too pigheaded to come with me."

"You didn't like Em's plans for you, Joe, so maybe you'll like mine better."

"What plans?"

Chuckie laughed. "I know this deep lake."

And I knew it was Geist Reservoir he was talking about then, where he already killed George.

The light flicked on and off of my face. "Poor Joe. Looks like he doesn't want to go for a swim."

"They'll still know it was you that did it," I said.

"Only if they find you, Joseph, only if they find you. And trust me, that just ain't going to happen. Not this time. Everything's going to be nice and quiet."

Which sounded like it was the barking dog that stopped his plans to drop George in the lake, because the fisherman heard the noise.

But I'd already had plenty too much of the water in the reservoir. So I said, "It'll be a bad risk for you to wheel me out of the hospital, Chuckie. You should just lock me in a closet when you go. That'd be safer."

"How do you figure that one, Joe?"

"They have security cameras all over. They'll know it was you from them. And the cops already gave the tapes from the house and lotto robberies to an expert, so he can prove it was you and George that did them."

"But I'm still walking around," Chuckie said. "I don't see any cops here. Do you see any cops here?"

"The cameras will just show some people in big hats," Emilee said. She showed me a bag she had with her. "We're not stupid."

"But you didn't wear any big hat when you came in to visit Freda the last two times, did you?"

She didn't answer, so it meant she didn't. I said, "They'll know it was you from that. They already know you're with Chuckie, so they'll get the both of you that way."

"Only if they find us, which ain't going to happen," Chuckie said. "The cops haven't even found where I really live yet. Not that I've left anything incriminating there."

And when he said all that, I heard things in his voice that weren't in the words. They reminded me how from his very earliest days Chuckie didn't like to leave loose ends that could catch him. So sure, he'd of cleaned the gun and the money out of wherever he really lived. And . . .

I said to Emi-lee, "He's going to kill you, too. You know that, don't you?"

She didn't answer for just a second. And that was enough for me to know it was crossing her mind for the first time now, even though what she said was, "Don't be stupid. We're in this together."

"Here we go again," Chuckie said. "Nice try, Joseph."

I said, "He's already killing Freda because she might wake up. Do you think he's going to take the chance that you ever might tell the cops what you know? He'll think, what if we both get caught and she decides to save herself?"

"Em knows we're a team. A dynamic duo."

But Emi-lee didn't say anything.

I said to her, "You haven't killed anybody yet. But when he kills Kelly's mom, you're a murderer just as much as he is. And you know what happens to murderers."

"Nothing happens. Not if you're smart," Chuckie said. "We're wasting time."

"Chuck . . . ?" Emi-lee said, and I could hear in her voice that she wasn't sure she wanted to do this anymore.

"Don't fall for his goddamned line, Em. For about my whole life I've seen Joe spin webs around women and before you know it they have their pants off."

"I only meant maybe I should take him out of here first."

"And do what? Fuck him?"

"If we're out of your way—"

"Cause you tried for that before." I could hear Chuckie's voice getting angrier and angrier. He said to me, "Why is it always you they want? Why not me? Because she tried to save you, Joe. She really did. No broad has ever tried to save me, but Em hatched up a whole plan to get you out of the room without knowing it was anything to do with me. And she'd have left you alive, too, only you didn't go for it."

"No woman ever saved you, Chuck?" Emi-lee said then, and she was angry now, too. "*I* fucking saved you."

"Well—"

"I gave you an alibi. Or don't you remember that? I even went out and bought a fucking dog to save your sorry ass."

"That's not what I meant."

"And this is the thanks I get? You sounding off, when all I'm trying to do is clear the room so you can do what you came here to do, and then get out quick without having to think about anything else?"

I heard Chuckie breathing extra hard at that. He was remembering that he ought to get on with it, but also he was angry as sin with her and me and his whole life of not getting the women he wanted and having loose ends. He could hardly talk from it all till finally he said, "Let's get this over and get out of here," like it was his own idea.

"At last," Emi-lee said.

"Put Joe out of his misery."

"What?" I said.

Chuckie gave another laugh. "Em has some sweet dreams for you in her bag, Joseph. In the form of half a brick. Farm girls have whole lots of talents. Just be glad she's going for your nut with it, and not your nuts. And know what? If she hits you hard enough to do the job the first time, there'll be hardly any blood. That's one of the good things about cracking people on the head. The first hit's free."

"But . . . But . . ." I tried to think of something to say.

Emi-lee looked in her bag for her brick and I felt how the needle came away from my neck. At the same time Chuckie turned to Kelly's mom and lifted the pillow he already had.

And I knew that if I was ever going to be alive again, it needed to be now.

I twisted as fast and hard in my chair as I could. I grabbed for Emi-lee's plastic needle to get it so at least I could defend myself.

What happened, though, was that by twisting so fast, I also spun the wheelchair. I missed grabbing Emi-lee's arm, but the handle of the chair hit her hard in the stomach and at the same time one of my crutches hit her head. I heard her go, "Ooof."

She pushed the chair away and it ran into the side of the bed, and somehow all that threw me onto the floor. My cast hit the ground and twisted my leg, and it hurt like holy hell.

All I could think to do was to roll over onto my back and so my leg would stop hurting. But doing that, I whacked my head on the floor. I saw stars. It was almost like night on the reservoir.

And then lights came on in the whole room. Was I dying?

I blinked to get used to them. Was I really seeing Kelly's mom sit up in her bed?

With a gun in her hand?

20

Kelly's mom shouted, "Police. Stop where you are."

At the same time doors opened from the hall and the bathroom and people rushed into the room. There were lots of them. And they had guns. I heard someone shout, "Charles Gardner I am arresting you . . ."

Three of them grabbed Chuckie, only he squirmed and twisted so much he shook them off. But then more got him again and he screamed. It was like wolves on a nature program, ganging up together on a moose no matter how much he fought.

I didn't see Emi-lee. She was behind where my head was pointed. I heard her swear, though.

And then I must of gone to sleep, because I stopped remembering what happened.

Where I woke up again I wasn't on Kelly's mom's floor at all, but I was in a bed.

I couldn't get my eyes open at first, because my lids were sticky. I tried to scrape the sticky stuff off with a hand, but there were tubes in the arm that got in the way. My other hand was OK, though, so I rubbed my eyes, only I also found there were bandages on my head. What was that about? You don't get head bandages for a broken leg.

With my eyes finally open I could see that I was in a hospital room, but not the same one as my own one on the eighth floor. So I didn't know where I was.

I didn't feel much like getting up to look around, though. Or even like sitting up. I was kind of numb inside my head, so I stayed lying down and I tried to work out what I could remember. But there wasn't really any of it after Chuckie's scream and Emi-lee's swear.

Chuckie's scream was awful. It sounded the way what happened to him looked—like being eaten from being pulled at and surrounded. Only it wasn't wolves, it was cops. Though maybe that's not so different.

And, Kelly's mom sat up. And she said she was a cop.

For a minute I tried to figure out how Kelly's mom could of trained to be a cop without me or even Kelly knowing she did it. But then I worked it out. The cop in the bed wasn't Kelly's mom at all. She was . . . a cop.

But then where was Freda?

My head hurt with the thinking about it. So I stopped.

I must of gone back to sleep because when I woke up again there were people in the room and I didn't hear them do it. I did hear that they were talking, but not what they were saying or who they were or how many.

For a minute it scared me. It felt like it was happening all over again—the people, the noise, the shouting. Only what I remembered this time wasn't Chuckie screaming or Emi-lee swearing but how much my leg hurt when I fell on the floor. That was horrible too.

But now my leg didn't hurt a lot. Some, but not much. My head hurt, though, which it never did before. Not a sharp hurt but in a numb kind. Truth is, pretty much all of me hurt at least a little bit. Like when you have the flu and all your muscles ache, even though some muscles ache worse than the others.

And one of the people in the room said, "Did he open his eyes?"

So I opened my eyes. And what I saw was a face right up close to mine and a bright light shining at me. I jumped and tried to back away, only I couldn't because I was lying in a bed.

"We have liftoff," somebody said. A woman.

And a man said, "You think he can hear us?"

So I said, "He can, if you mean me."

"What? What was that?" somebody said, but it was farther away and I couldn't tell if it was one of the people who already talked or not.

So I said, "Hi."

"He is awake," the man said.

"Time to make the calls." That was the woman. Her voice sounded familiar now.

I opened my eyes wider and I turned my head now. And I saw three people in the room and the closest was the woman who was my doctor, Dr. Jepson. So I said to her, "I feel funny. Am I sick?"

She said some things back, or somebody else did, or maybe they all did, but I was tired again and didn't have the energy to sort it out. So I closed my eyes to rest them.

When I woke up again it was Cayenne sitting by my bed, but I could also see Steponkus was in a chair beside her. They didn't see that I was awake at first, because they were talking to each other. But even sitting down, it was funny how one was so big and the other so little. I laughed.

Cayenne turned to me. "Joe?"

"Hi."

The both of them moved their chairs closer. "How are you feeling?" Cayenne asked.

"OK, I guess."

"They called this morning to say you were out of it."

My eyes were tired again, but I thought if I kept talking they'd know I was still awake. "Out of what?"

"You've been unconscious for more than a day, Mr. Prince," Steponkus said.

"I have?"

"You fractured your skull on the floor when you fell out of your wheelchair," Cayenne said.

"I did?"

"And your leg broke again."

I remembered how much my leg hurt. I said, "Oh."

"But they put you back together, Mr. Prince," Steponkus said. "Good as new. And all at IPD's expense, even though you weren't in police custody at the time."

"Not in custody, but smack dab in the middle of a police operation without having been told about it or having been given the opportunity not to take part," Cayenne said.

"An operation that successfully resolved the crimes he had been accused of," Steponkus said.

"An operation in which he fractured his skull and broke his leg."

"We are paying for it all," Steponkus said.

"You'd be in court before you could blink if you even thought about not paying for it. Jeez, you guys are such sports to take responsibility for the consequences of your actions," Cayenne said.

"What are you complaining about, Cayenne?" Steponkus said.

"But for your 'operation,' my client would be out of this hospital by now. He'd be on his crutches and probably at home dancing the tango with Kelly."

"And his mother-in-law might well be dead and with Charles Gardner walking the streets trying to decide who to kill next."

There was more that they argued to each other, but with my

eyes closed to rest them, I didn't get a word in edgeways.

When I woke up again Kelly was there.

"Joe?"

I felt better already just seeing her. I moved to try to sit up. I wanted to get close. I wanted to touch her. "Is it really you?"

She said, "Easy, Joe, easy," but she must of known what I wanted because she tipped herself out of her chair and onto part of the bed and put her arms around me, as far as they would go with me lying down.

There is nothing that feels as good as that felt then.

"Oh, Kell," I said.

"I was so worried, Joe."

"About what?"

"About you, you big lunk."

And then I remembered how Cayenne said I was unconscious for a day. I said, "Oh." Only then I remembered I wasn't the only unconscious one. "How's your mom?"

"As a matter of fact, she's better."

"You mean she's awake now at last?"

"Not awake yet," Kelly said, shaking her head, "but they think she will be soon."

"Oh yeah. The protocol. I guess it worked."

"There was no protocol or operation, Joe," Kelly said. "All they did to Momma was move her to a different room."

I didn't understand at first. "But Dr. Hallarson said . . ."

Kelly must of seen it on my face because she said, "It was all a trap for Chuckie."

"It was?"

"You remember how they let him out of jail the other day?"

"I sure do. It was on the TV."

"Well, when they let him go they followed him. And that's how they knew that he sent his girlfriend in to visit Momma."

"Lee," I said. "Emi-lee."

"What?"

"Go on."

"Well, his girlfriend came in to visit Momma to find out if she would wake up. So the police arranged for a doctor to come into Momma's room when the girlfriend was there to say he was going to do something so Momma would wake up the next day. They figured that would make Chuckie have to come in that night. And that's what happened."

After a minute I said, "So there was no protocol?"

"No, Joe."

"But there was a police operation?"

"And they caught Chuckie."

"So your mom didn't wake up tomorrow? Or . . ." I'd lost track of the days a little. "Or whenever?"

"She's not awake, Joe, but she is better."

"She is?"

"They don't know why. Maybe something about moving her to a different room stimulated something. But they told me they expect her to wake up soon. There are signs of it. Today. Tomorrow. It could be any time now."

"I'm so glad, Kell."

"And I won't ever forget how you went down there and talked to her all through the night, Joe. Even though . . ."

She didn't say it, but I knew she was thinking in her head, *even though you hate the old witch and she hates you.*

"I did it for you," I said.

"I know, Joe. I know."

"And because if she did wake up from me talking, maybe she would like me better and let us all be a family together."

"I'm going to talk to her, Joe. Things have got to be different now." And she squeezed my hand, and I squeezed hers back.

Then she said, "I am so sorry about you getting hurt again.

But I just had to say it was OK for them to do it, Joe, and not to tell you in case you gave it away. If I didn't let them do it, then nobody was safe from Chuckie. Not Momma. Not you. Not me. Probably not even Little Joe. Do you forgive me?"

"Forgive you?"

"For saying they could do it."

"Sure."

"Really? Because I never cried so much in my life as when you didn't wake up after it."

"Really?"

"Oh yeah."

"So we are back together now? For real? For good?"

"We are."

"You and me and Little Joe . . ." I frowned. "Where is he?"

"He's asleep in Momma's room. Her new one. A nurse there is looking after him so I could come up to see you. But I'm going to go back down there now, Joe."

"You are?"

"I don't want Momma to wake up and me not be there."

After a minute I could see that. "I can see that."

"You know, I think maybe the reason she's going to wake up was all the talking to her you did. Maybe it took a little time to sink in."

I thought about that, and how glad I was if what I did could make Kelly happier. Then I said, "Really?"

Only by then Kelly was already at the door of my room on her way out. But before she left she blew me a kiss.

That made me really happy. We were going to be together again. At last.

And then I was in Kelly's mom's room in the hospital, only Kelly was there too this time.

Freda was in her bed and not awake yet, even though it could be any time now. I said to Kelly, "I love you so much."

"I love you too, Joe."

"I really am more grown up now and more mature too. I've worked hard at it and didn't give in to Linda or Lee or any of them."

"I know, Joe. But it won't matter so much now," Kelly said.

"It won't?"

"Because I'm not going to leave you alone anymore, no matter whose funeral it is."

"Oh Kelly." And my leg was a lot better, because I could get up out of my chair, which maybe wasn't even a wheelchair now. I went to her, and she went to me. "Oh Kelly," I said again.

"Oh Joe," she said.

And I pulled at her shirt, and she pulled at my belt, and a minute later we were there on the floor, only it wasn't cold or hard like a lot of floors, so maybe we had the clothes under us to make it softer.

And then we were . . . doing it.

Only there was a noise in the room. I looked up and I could see it was Freda sitting up in her bed. Kelly didn't notice and was oooing, like she does, and ahhhing.

"Freda?" I said.

And then I saw Freda had a gun. Only when I looked again I saw it wasn't a gun at all, but a finger she was pointing at me. She said, "Thank you for telling me about Shoeless Joe Jackson, and for protecting me in case Chuckie came to kill me."

"That's OK, Freda," I said.

"And thanks for waking me up, Joe. We're a real family now." Then she lay back down on her bed where I couldn't see her.

And I lay back down on Kelly. Truth is, that's about the most comfortable place to lie down that I can think of in the whole wide world.

ACKNOWLEDGMENTS

Many people helped me with facts, encouragement, tolerance and distraction as I buried myself in Joe Prince's voice and mind, but I particularly want to thank Chloe Homewood for her singular contribution to this novel.

MZL
April 2007

ABOUT THE AUTHOR

Michael Z. Lewin has been writing mysteries for more than thirty years. His novels and stories have been published in many countries, winning awards in Japan and Germany as well as the US where his work has also been nominated for Edgars three times. Raised in Indianapolis, Mike now lives in England. Too old to function credibly on a basketball court these days, he gardens on his patio and sings in a community choir. He also has the most fabulous children and grandchildren as there ever were. His Web site is www.MichaelZLewin.com.